Somebody Else's Summer

Clarke, Irwin & Company Limited/Toronto/Vancouver 1973

Somebody
TED WOOD Else's
Summer

contents

acknowledgements

The following stories were broadcast on c.b.c.:
A Present for Alice   1962
American Primitive   1970
The Cucumber Contract   1971
Kinder than the Sea   1971
Got to Travel On   1972
Out of the Rain (prev. title: George)   1973

for Mary

Somebody Else's Summer

Somebody
Else's
Summer

A boat-tailed grackle floated down from an apple tree and pecked at a dab of caviare some guest had dropped and then attempted to tread out of sight into the faultless lawn.

Frazer watched, amused, wondering if the bird cared what it was eating. "Decadent capitalist bird," he said.

No one heard him, except for the waiter, alone on his own side of the bar with his rows of bottles and the ice-filled chest of champagne. The filtered light in the marquee gave an orange tint to his young, pale face. Frazer glanced at him and wondered what he was thinking, young, fit and alien, standing in the shadows while a rich girl married a rich man amid music and the officious popping of champagne corks.

It was good champagne too, Frazer reflected, reading the label nearest to him. No sugary domestic substitutes for his daughter's wedding. He smiled into his own glass of ginger ale.

3

And so it should be—she deserved it. At twenty-three she had the beauty he remembered in her mother on their wedding day.

He finished his ginger ale and the bartender moved forward at once, champagne ready. Frazer shook his head and smiled again. "Never touch the stuff," he said.

Out on the patio the orchestra had started playing something sentimental and the guests were dancing. It was time to face them again, he decided. He must dance with the bride.

He set down his glass and moved out, blinking and narrowing his eyes against the sunlight. Funny, he thought, the action had become automatic over the years. He had forgotten until this very minute that he had once practised the look, greedy for the authority that lines around his eyes added to the shiny new wings over his left pocket, those wings whose newness had stubbornly persisted even after a soaking in English brown ale.

He smiled at the memory. How many years ago was that anyway? More than half his lifetime. He found he was standing, staring through his narrowed eyes at a startled wedding guest. He shook his head. "Sorry."

He stepped quickly by. He must keep his mind on the present, on this golden, gift-wrapped day, the final evidence that he himself had once been young. The boys were long since married and gone. Now there was only Alison, the youngest of the three, a peacetime child with no inherited taint of those fearful nights in black, indifferent skies.

He moved through the guests to the edge of the patio. His daughter and her husband of a few hours were dancing together and the ladies in the crowd were making cooing noises. Frazer repressed a quick bubble of laughter. It was such a perfect cliché, all of it, so Victorian, as fragrant and as dated as violet cachous.

The dance ended, the groom bowed to Alison and led her from the patio. The crowd applauded, politely, as if to a good rally at the country club tennis match.

Frazer felt swamped by the predictability of it all. He looked around for something human, something to demonstrate the intensity of his feeling. How could he show this clutter of canapé-nibbling middle-aged people that this young woman was precious and vital, that this day was a monument?

He noticed the rose, long-stemmed and perfect, lacking only

the florist's artful aerosol spray with a dew to render it the supreme cliché of the day. He went over to the bush, treading on lesser border flowers, the sweet alyssum and portulaca and picked the rose, ripping the long stem from the reluctant bush with a flourish that stripped the bark down one side. He pricked his finger but did not feel the discomfort. Nor did he acknowledge the gasps of surprise that followed his action. If people chose to censure him, that was their problem.

He took his flower to the edge of the circle of friends surrounding his daughter and her husband. He waited patiently until the conversation faltered, then he handed her the flower.

"Daddy!" She almost squealed it, the way she would once have squealed at one of his jokes. "Mummy will just *kill* you."

"I wanted you to have it," he said.

"Well, it certainly is gorgeous, isn't it, Harry."

"Beautiful," Harry said gravely, his eyes on his bride.

Frazer looked at the young man and wanted to say, "How would you know? It doesn't have a price tag on it."

Alison said, "You should wear it, Daddy."

She was shortening the stem, working with tanned fingers made strong by golf and tennis and riding. He watched as she bent the stem back and forth until it frayed in two.

"But I have a flower," he protested laughingly.

"You had a flower," she corrected, pushing the rose into the top pocket of his rented jacket. "You gave it to Mrs. Roudy-busch at the receiving line, remember."

She fussed and patted the rose until it was primped up to its most perfect angle. "There," she said, with a tiny set of her head as she viewed her handiwork. He was reminded again of her mother. She had the same confidence, the same instinctive knowledge of what was right.

The music began again, this time a more modern beat, something Latin American, from the early sixties. Frazer wished it were a waltz but he went ahead anyway. "Harry, if you will release the bride, I promise I'll take good care of her. Mrs. Graham, may I have the honour?"

His daughter giggled. "It's so funny to be Mrs. Graham."

"You've just exchanged one good Scottish name for another," Frazer said.

He led her the few steps to the dance area and they set out,

Alison moving exquisitely, Frazer skirting the edges of the rhythms, out of his element. It was not a success.

Over her shoulder he saw Harry Graham summon a waiter with a practised finger and take two glasses of champagne which he held, staring patiently at his bride's back.

Through the French doors of the house came a couple of elderly women, powdery and elegant, shepherded by his ex-wife, a tall graceful woman of about forty-five. He watched her come down the steps of her home, a house he had been inside only once. She paused beside the groom and spoke to him, not smiling now that her charges were released. The young man answered, nodding in the direction of Frazer.

Her eyes followed the young man's glance and met Frazer's. He gave a half smile and a nod of recognition but saw her lips tighten. It was the rose, he supposed, Daphne was angry about one lousy rose.

The orchestra finished the tune and began another, still at the same tempo. Frazer said, "I guess that's our cue, Ali."

She said, "All right."

He escorted her back to her husband who asked unsmilingly, "Have fun?"

"Yes," Ali said and accepted the glass of champagne held out for her.

Frazer watched Daphne, waiting for her attack. It took the form of a smile, wide enough to fool a person standing even a yard away. She put her hand on his arm and hissed "Are you out of your mind?"

He carried on the pantomime for the sake of the bystanders, smiling and patting her hand. "Since when has dancing with the bride been a form of madness?"

Daphne drew him away from the young couple, unobtrusively but firmly. "I'm talking about the rose. I saw you from the window. Trampling through the flower beds, ripping down a prize rose bush. What's the matter, you promised you wouldn't drink."

"I had ginger ale," Frazer said, "ginger ale, even to toast the bride."

"Says you," she said and Frazer felt himself dazed with a sense of time travel. Nobody in the world said "Says you" anymore. It was dead, like the generation of movie stars who had made that kind of language popular, like the generation of young men who had imitated them in pubs close to bomber bases in England. It was dead as the summer in which he had married this foundry foreman's daughter.

He said, "I don't think I've heard anyone say that since the war."

"The war." Her voice knocked the word down and dragged it across the ground. "The war and your medal and your two tours of operations. Let's not go through all that again."

"*You* never went through it," he said reasonably.

"Don't be so tiresome." She didn't care that Alison heard her.

Alison carefully did not, making a neat quarter-turn on her heel, turning her back on them completely.

Frazer looked down at the rose in his pocket, filling his mind with its perfection, letting the thought push away his feelings of inadequacy. Daphne's toughness was unnecessary, some kind of a joke on her if only she could see it.

She was saying, "For your daughter's sake at least, try and act like an adult for these few hours. And don't drink."

He looked at her, not speaking. Then he gave a quick shake to his wrist, throwing off her restraining hand. He turned away from her, away from the whole lot of them and walked down the lawn.

For a moment he was drawn to the marquee, to the comfort of the long rows of bottles behind the bar but he mastered the feeling and went on by, sensing Daphne's eyes on his back like twin daggers.

He walked in a straight line, deliberately straight to confound Daphne and her ugly suspicions, coming at last to the crunching red gravel of the driveway. Here he turned, following the driveway to the area back of the coach-house where the guests' Cadillacs and Mercedes and Jaguars were parked.

He found himself sitting in his own car. Sunlight had warmed the seats and through the open windows he could hear birds singing and the distant orchestra playing a tune from the fifties. He felt calm and remote, away from the temperaments and the pressures of the day. His hand, acting like a creature with its own intelligence, opened the glove compartment and took out the bottle, a cheap, flat pint of rye. He had promised he would not drink at Alison's wedding and he would not. But this was his own private place, there was no wedding going on here. Slowly he grasped the cap and twisted it off, enjoying the pleasurable little tug as the seal ripped.

Then he drank, an economical movement of head and wrist that threw down four ounces in a single gesture.

He lowered the bottle and screwed the cap back on. Already he regretted taking the drink. He always did. Once the tightness left his face and his brain became comfortable again inside his skull it was always the same.

He sat back, pressing the flat, warm bottle between his palms, listening to the music and the birdsong. Today really was a perfect day for Ali's wedding. Even allowing for Daphne's bitchiness about the silly rose, it was a perfect day, a perfect setting. How different from his own wedding day. Daphne had been beautiful of course. Even in her WAAF uniform with her hair in the unflattering roll style the girls had been wearing then.

Frazer smiled wryly at the memory. The setting had been so very different. No marquee on the lawn. No champagne. Instead there had been a barrel of dull wartime beer, set on two chairs in the passageway of the terrace house in Huddersfield. And Daphne's mother, huge old Amy sobbing into her handkerchief.

He unscrewed the cap of the bottle and sipped again, thoughtfully. The tone of the day had been set by something Amy had said the first time he went home with Daphne. "Ee, lad, we've never 'ad an officer in the 'ouse before." An officer. A sprog pilot officer, commissioned along with a hundred others to refill the holes being shot in the RCAF every night. He tried to tell them that, without sounding too pessimistic about his own future but they had preferred to consider him an officer, one of "Them."

He reclosed the bottle and pushed it back into the glove compartment. It was so mystifyingly English. The holy trinity in Daphne's Dad's life was 't foundry, 't pub and 't missus. They couldn't really understand the social restlessness in their daughter. Why had she joined the marginally more classy

WAAFs rather than the "jolly good pals" ATs along with other girls from her street? Why had she taken up with a Canadian officer rather than a nice English lance corporal? And why did she sound "posh" when she talked? It had puzzled her father. He hadn't really understood her, and he hadn't really trusted Frazer. His farewell words on their wedding day had been typical. To his daughter a casual "Well, ta-ra then," and to his new son-in-law, officer, gentleman, provider of Sweet Cap cigarettes he had said only "Tek care of 'er." Frazer shook his head in fond recollection of the old man. What would he think of today's "Do"? In salute to his memory he took out the mickey again and finished it in two swallows. He got out of his car and headed back up the driveway, relaxed and happier than he had been since he knew the wedding was to happen.

The heat drained him as he walked. The driveway stretched out like a runway. The thought amused him and he made a little game of planning his approach, the long slow curve into the pattern and then the straight letdown. Flaps down. Wheels down, back and back on the throttles, don't let her stall, let her down lightly on injured wings, bringing back work for the riggers and armourers and for the ambulance crew that waited at dispersal. Letting down with holes in the fuselage and empty bomb bays and a dead gunner in the rear turret, letting down sweet and slow so they could fly again and get on with the war and never mind these rumours that there would be peace sometime, somewhere.

He collided with a couple of people who were standing talking on the grass verge. "I beg your pardon," he said and added the words he had always uttered when the bomb aimer reported "Bombs Gone": "Nothing personal." The woman, a well-kept dowager in her fifties, snorted. The man, who might have been her son, chuckled. Frazer narrowed his eyes at him and the boy turned away.

He went back to the patio. The crowd had thinned and Alison and her husband were nowhere to be seen. He went to the best man, a long-haired and elegant youth cut from the same expensive cloth as the bridegroom. He was standing with one of the bridesmaids whispering something that was making the girl laugh a knowing laugh. "Pardon me," Frazer said. The best man looked at him with the insulting politeness of the young. "Why, hello, Mr. Frazer." "Hi," Frazer said. "Did you see where the happy couple went?" He saw the glances exchanged by the boy and the bridesmaid and wished he hadn't said anything so trite.

"Yes, sir. They went in to change. They're leaving soon."

"Thank you." Frazer smiled at the bridesmaid. "Sorry to butt in."

"Don't mention it," she said.

He turned away, ignoring her laugh. It had nothing to do with him. Nothing she could do or say had anything to do with him.

His feet seemed to lead him to the marquee. The same waiter was there, holding what might have been the same bottle of champagne. Frazer went up to him, smiling. "I've changed my mind," he said.

The waiter's mouth creased for a microsecond, conspiratorially. He held up the champagne bottle but Frazer shook his head. "No, Scotch please, straight up."

He watched while the man poured a neat professional ounce and a quarter. His tongue seemed to swell in his mouth, choking his words. "And I'll take one for, er, for my wife," he said.

The waiter made the second drink, not looking at him. Frazer took them up, feeling the strength radiate through the glass into his hands and shaking arms. He nodded thanks and turned away. Not far away. He would do more business here, before the young people came out of the house.

He drank the first one as quickly as he could. Then he got rid of the glass and stood holding the second drink as if he didn't really care for it. By now he could feel his own whisky working on him, dislocating the world to the other side of a transparent distorting bubble that surrounded him. He kept his head clear by focusing very hard on the bottles behind the bar while he finished his drink, demonstrating the neatness of his co-ordination to a guest who paused in the doorway of the marquee to stare at him. The Scotch was smooth and good and reassuring. He took the few steps back to the bar and held out his glass, not speaking. The waiter poured him the same efficient ounce and a quarter and Frazer signalled with his finger for a double. The man looked at him, trying to assess which course of action would cause the least trouble. Frazer met his glance with open eyes as firm as two stones. The man gave a tiny shrug and added another shot to the glass. "Thank you," Frazer said.

He heard a burst of applause from the patio and turned to check the reason. Alison was back outside, in her going away outfit, a pretty blue pant suit. She stood, arm in arm with her groom, talking to Daphne and Daphne's new husband, Bill Masters. Frazer watched them for a moment then swallowed his drink and set out for the patio, moving his legs as if they were blocks of wood. He paused as he reached the end of the bar and picked up the nearest full bottle, shoving it into the left pocket of his jacket. The waiter called out "Hey, Mister," but Frazer ignored him and stumped out into the sunlight. He could hear the groom saying, "And you're not going to find out. We're not telling *anybody*." And then the little group laughed the relieved hahahas of social equals.

Frazer had decided days ago what his parting words would be. They came out clumsily, like gulps of liquor from an upturned bottle. "Harry, asmy own fa-in-law, said-a-me. Tek care of 'er." His Yorkshire accent was accurate and the playful punch he landed on Harry's jaw was only a touch too hard.

He saw Daphne's mouth open, and then Bill's, and felt their hands at each of his elbows. Still he managed to deliver his speech, his compliments both to Ali and to this tense angry bitch at his elbow. "Thou are thy Mu's glass, and sheinthee calls back the lully April of her prime," he quoted.

Alison was crying. He couldn't understand it. Why cry? Why cry in front of this crowd of free-loading has-beens? He tried to comfort her but no words came and Daphne's husband's voice, cultured and smooth as oil on troubled waters was pouring over the whole audience. "Touch too much sun, Ian, old boy. Come on into the house and lie down." And Daphne's staccato counterpoint. "Drunk as a lord. How humiliating." All the words of all the guests came to him, hanging in the air like paper streamers he could catch and read at his leisure. "Look, he's got a bottle of gin in his pocket." "Did you see him picking the rose?" and the ultimate insult, "Who is he?"

11

The world was beginning to spin and he knew he would be sick and he knew he would recover. As the faces blurred, trailing trace-lines of anger behind them he felt only sadness. Not for himself—hell, he understood. He was standing right in the centre of the world and he *knew*. He was sorry only that so many rich and clever and beautiful people like Daphne and Bill and their friends could get so excited about an incident on a day that didn't belong to them. The day, the year, the lifetime was out of their hands. Why was it that he alone of all his generation could accommodate the fact that this was not his day, this was somebody else's summer.

As his consciousness deserted him he made one last brave attempt to put his wisdom into words, phrasing it as the answer to the last shrill question. Biting off each word to isolate the treacherous esses he said, "I used to be the bride's father."

Out of the Rain

The afternoon light had dimmed to a sulphurous yellow and a sudden frightened wind had sprung up, spinning the roadside maples. Dust eddied along the shoulder of the road and a cloud of fragments tore loose from the load of straw to fly over George's head and away down the long concession that stretched in front of his tractor.

Then the rain began to fall, each drop hard and flat. Within seconds George was soaked, his shirt and work pants black with water. His hair darkened too, clinging close to his round, small head. He drove on uncaring, knowing the straw would stay dry under the tarpaulin his father and brother Walt had tied over it. He stopped where the concession crossed the highway and waited, looking both ways with an earnest ticking motion of his head until the road was clear. Then he pulled across and put the tractor into third gear again as he started up the slow hill that led past Murdoch's pasture.

He became aware that the tractor was labouring at the throttle setting he had given it, the setting he always gave it on this stretch of the road home.

He reached down and pulled the lever a little farther back— not too far, mustn't let her rattle. Dad said it shouldn't rattle, not ever.

The labouring did not improve. George narrowed his eyes again and thought about it. He had a hundred and seventeen bales on the wagon but it was straw. This tractor would draw that many *hay* bales without going slow like this. His hand strayed to the throttle again but he did not open it farther and presently the motor died.

He switched off the ignition as he had been instructed and put the brake on, tapping it into the lock with the toe of his boot. Then, leaving the engine in gear, he stepped down and took a slow walk around the wagon. The rain still spouted down, bouncing knee-high as every drop exploded on the warm tarred surface of the road. And then he saw the trouble. The back tire was flat, torn half off the rim with a frill of tattered inner tube protruding like a black tongue sticking out at his discomfiture. George looked at it and rubbed his head. His Dad would be mad about that. His shallow memory prompted him with cues of a message he had been given. His Dad had said to watch something. Watch the tire. Now he remembered the whole warning—watch the tire, it's blistered, don't keep going on it and tear it all up.

Behind him, over the steady hiss of the rain, he heard laughter. It came and went in little puffs of sound as whoever was laughing ran towards him.

He turned and looked. Two boys his own age and a girl were running down the road from the direction of the camp ground that Mrs. Dickson had opened up alongside her sugarbush by the crick.

One of the boys was black. George couldn't remember seeing a black boy up close before and he stared at him as the three of them ran towards him.

They reached his wagon and the girl shouted, "C'mon under

16

here." The boys laughed and the black boy said, "Hey, yeah," and the three of them dropped to their knees and crept under the wagon bed out of the rain.

The girl looked out at George, laughing from a wide, happy mouth. "Why don't you come out of the rain?" she asked.

"Huh?" George said and the girl began again, "I said why don't you . . . ."

The white boy interrupted her. "Ackwards-bay," he said slowly, mouthing the syllables with a wide movement of his jaws, as if the sounds were hot.

The girl stopped and looked at him for a moment, then nodded, and stopped laughing.

"I didn't realize," she said.

The boy waved at George. "Hey, man, c'mon."

Obediently, George crouched down and came in under the wagon. He was still wet and the road was streaming but it felt better not to have the water beating on his head.

He stared at the girl. She was pretty, like a girl in a commercial. Her hair was wet and so was her shirt. George could see her nipples jutting through the thin material and he stared at them. He couldn't remember ever seeing a girl's nipples before.

He realized the white boy was talking to him. "Your tire's flat, d'you know that?"

George nodded. "It tore all up," he said.

"All to Heeeeeeell," the black boy said and the three of them started laughing. George looked at each of them in turn, trying to see why they were laughing so hard. There was nothing funny anywhere. It was raining and his tire was all tore up and they were sitting on wet road. There was nothing funny. He looked at the bundles they were carrying. Each of them had a haversack and the white boy had a funny-shaped box with a handle. Maybe that was what made them laugh.

He said, "What you got inside there?"

The boy laughed. "Direct little devil, aren't you," he said.

George smiled because they all smiled. "Wha's inside?" he repeated finally.

The girl said, "It's a guitar." She spoke kindly, the way Miss Roberts at school used to. The other boys stopped laughing when she spoke and the white one said, "There's music inside there."

"Yeah?" George felt himself grinning. He knew they were funning him.

"Yeah," the boy said. "You wanna see?"

"All right," George said.

The boy took the case on his knees and moved farther under the wagon, farther away from the hissing rain. There was even less headroom under the center of the wagon and he had to lie almost flat on his back, his head pillowed on his pack as he opened the case and took out the guitar.

It was dark and shiny. George looked at it and knew he mustn't touch it.

The boy handed the box aside and the girl took it, closing it carefully and keeping it in her arms away from the wetness of the road beneath them.

"Play something," she said and George could hardly hear her for the beating of the rain. "Play me a blues for a rainy day."

The boy with the guitar didn't answer. He lay for a moment, then he wiped his hand on the comparatively dry part of his shirt under his other arm, a quick dipping motion that George thought was going to make the music.

And then he started to play. And George felt the little hairs on the back of his head growling up straight as he listened. He felt his belly muscles tighten and his heart swell up in his chest until he could hardly breathe. His head would not stay still, it weaved back and forth to the music, carrying his short neck and wide strong shoulders back and forth, in and out of the sound of the music, in and out of the sound of the rain.

He heard the black boy say, "Hey, man, you got yourself a real live fan f' Chrissakes."

Then the music stopped.

George said, "Wha'd'ya stop for?"

"Had to, man, there ain't no more," the boy told him. He was smiling, fingers ready to play more, head comfortable against the pack, back flat on the warm, wet road. The black boy was kneeling next to him, head bent under the lowness of the wagon bed. "Here, let a soul brother play," he said and the boy

18

handed him the guitar as freely as if it were a bottle or something else of no consequence.

George watched as the black fingers with their pink under-
sides stung a spurt of sound from the strings. And then the
music had hold of him again, carrying him away as surely
as rainwater was carrying away the dross of summer from
the shoulder of the road. He sat and rocked and slapped
his legs with his hands and as he did so he felt the bump in
the pocket and he remembered that he could make music too.
He interrupted his rocking and swaying long enough to push
his hands deep into his pocket and take out the fifty-cent
harmonica he had found on the school bus last year when he
still went to school.

He took it in his hands and looked into it, at the damp dust
that clogged the holes in it. He could see the boys and girl
looking at one another with the look the kids on the bus had
worn, not quite laughing but the corners of their mouths tucked
down tight so they wouldn't.

He didn't care. The music had him like a horse has a rider.

He raised the harmonica to his lips, and in the moment
before he closed his eyes he saw the girl cover her ears with her
hands, laughing unashamedly.

George didn't care. He took the tiny instrument between his
lips and tore from it the gasping snorts of joy that had
soothed him so many times when nothing else could still the
mumblings in his head. He swayed and rocked but now his own
sounds rode with the guitar sounds, lifting him like some huge
bird that could carry him and the wagon and the tractor and
the hundred and seventeen bales of straw as if they were nothing,
could float them up and through the other side of the sky.

He heard the boy saying, "Can you believe that? An honest
to God blues." And the black boy echoing the surprise, "Believe
it man, this dude is gooood."

Then the guitar stopped and George stopped with it, wrapping up the sky and the wind and the rainclouds into one big
note that felt good down through his teeth and into his chest.

He opened his eyes and found the girl clapping her hands.
"You play great," she said.

19

George shook his head. "No. You wanna hear Walt play. He can play Red River Valley an ever'thing."

The white boy said, "That good, eh?"

George said, "Yes," and wondered why they were laughing again. They were funny people—the one boy's hair was as long as the girl's and the black boy was dressed in a red shirt and pants that were purple where they weren't soaked through.

George looked at the girl again. She was laughing less than the boys, just a big smile really. She had set down the guitar case across her knees and taken hold of the front of her shirt with both forefingers and thumbs and was holding it away from herself so that he couldn't see her nipples any more, drying her shirt.

She said, "Can you play tunes?"

George did not raise his eyes from her fingers and she repeated the question. "Hello in there," she said. "I say can you play tunes?"

George looked at her face again. "No. I can't play tunes. I can't play it, Walt says."

The girl was beginning to say something, not smiling now but serious. And then George cut her off, finding words to explain what he felt. "I can't play it," he said. "But I can make it sing."

The white boy gave a sudden excited whistle and sat up so quickly he almost hit his head on the underside of the wagon. "Jesus, man, that's beautiful"—he waved his hand at the other two—"like, that's really beautiful."

George wondered why he was so excited, and why the black boy had lowered his head over the guitar and was shaking it slowly back and forth, squeezing his eyes together as if he was going to cry. But he did not. Instead he struck another ring from the guitar. "Make it sing again," he said softly.

George could not have disobeyed.

He put the harmonica to his mouth and tore the first note loose from it, his eyes sinking closed with the weight of his joy. He could hear the girl singing, a low song with no words, and he could feel the guitar striking fire from his bones and the warm rags of sound from his own harmonica wrapping all of them in happiness.

20

He played until his mouth was sore at the corners and the little pain had started biting his lips. And then the music stopped. First the singing, then the guitar, and then his own music withered and stopped as he opened his eyes and stared out from under the wagon at the sunlit, steaming roadway.

The white boy was lying on his side, staring out over the top of his pack, forward, past the tractor wheels. "Someone's stopped," he said.

The black boy reached out towards the girl. "Gimme that box," he said. "Let's git."

The girl handed the guitar case to him. "I don't want to. I dig this," she said.

The white boy said, "Yeah, some big dude. He's coming back."

The black boy tumbled the guitar into the case. "Let's git," he said again. "I don't dig some cat ' can play Red River Valley, kickin' my black ass."

The three of them began to scramble their way out from under the wagon. George came after them, puzzling why the boy had said "ass" in front of the girl. His father had said he mustn't say "ass" in front of girls.

The harmonica was still in his hand and it tapped on the wet roadway as he came out on hands and knees to find himself facing Walter's boots and the legs of Walter's green pants.

"Hi, Walter," he said. And Walter told him, "Get up."

The two boys and the girl were putting their packs on. They were standing by the back of the wagon but Walter went over to them. "What's going on?" he asked them, his red face angry under the peaked green cap he had bought at the Co-op.

The black boy said nothing. The white boy shook his head so the shoulder-length hair fell straight to dry in the sun. "Just sheltering from the rain, brother," he said.

Walt was mad. George knew it. He could tell by the jumpiness in his own throat. Walt was mad.

"You're not my brother. You're a long haired hippy and you been messing with this boy." The white boy and the girl both said "No we haven't," together, but the black boy said nothing.

Walter said, "I ought to call the p'lice. Lookit his mouth. His mouth's cut."

George put his fingers up to his mouth and looked at them. There was a little pinkness on them. He wondered why.

"Lookit. He's bleeding," Walter said. "Somebody hit him." Walter looked at George, holding his chin and tilting his face so he could see the tiny cuts on the corners of the mouth. "What happened?" he asked in a voice that made George shivery.

"We sat under the wagon," George said. He wished Walter would let go of his chin, it made talking difficult. Walter said nothing and did not release his face, but stared into it angrily as if it were a mirror and he were practising his angry face. "Out of the rain," George said finally.

He could see that his three friends were going to leave him and he wanted them to stay, he wanted the music to go on some more.

Walter let go of his chin suddenly, almost throwing his face aside as he turned to the three young people. "You ought to be ashamed, picking on a boy that don't know what's going on," he said. He was blazing angry. "Making fun of him, laughing at him while he makes a damn fool of himself with that there mouth organ." He turned to George and whipped the harmonica from his hand and threw it away over the fence into the Murdoch's pasture. George wailed "Walter . . ." but stood still, not knowing what made his brother so mad.

And then the girl was angry too. She stepped up in front of Walter and shouted into his face. "You're sick. You know that. You're a stupid ignorant bully."

And then everyone was shouting. Walter was shouting and the two boys were shouting, standing one pace away from him, either side of him so that he had to swing his head from one to the other as he shouted down their expressions of contempt and hatred.

The black boy kept saying, "He's a natural musician, man, a natural blues musician," and it was this that made Walter angriest of all. "You think that's funny, eh? Him honking away making a monkey of himself while you laugh at him, you bastards. Get away from here, get the hell away."

And as George watched, they left, first the white boy, then the black and finally the girl, pausing only to spit at Walter's feet. The three of them walked away, shoulders hunched, down the steaming road while Walter stood, his hands in his belt, looking after them.

George watched until they had reached the county road and had swung around limply to hang their thumbs against the city-bound traffic. Then he turned to find Walter walking away to the flat tire of the wagon. He felt his earlier nervousness come back as he walked to join his brother who was stooping, hands on his knees, staring at the ruin of the tire. "It bust," he explained.

Walter straightened up, easing his shoulders as if some load had just been taken from them. "Yeah, I can see that," he said, kindly. He reached out his hand and ruffled George's short, crisp hair. "You're crazy as a hoot owl George, y'know that?" he said.

He turned away to the pickup, calling over his shoulder, "Come on now, gimme a hand with this jack. We got work to do, not like some folks."

And George could feel his back and arms growing eager at the thought of working on the wheel and he laughed, once, a shred of the same sound he had made earlier with his harmonica.

Kinder
than
the Sea

Away to the left of the canoe, close to the shore with its slabs of colour, red rock and yellowing foliage laid on black water, a bird surfaced, puncturing the skin of the lake with the cleverness of a conjuring trick. In the bow of the canoe Blake stopped making his short, inept paddle strokes and waved towards the bird. "Tha's a loon, id'nt it?"

Hargreaves changed sides with his paddle, correcting the swing of the canoe. "Right," he said to Blake's back. He had found himself talking more and more in monosyllables since the outing began the day before. There was something challenging about the mulled-cider warmth of Blake's Cornish speech, an implicit reproach for the fact that his sister, Hargreaves' wife, did not speak the same way any more. Twelve years of living in Canada had broken the back of her vowels and chilled the consonants.

"Cormorants 'll dive," Blake said. "Go under for, oh, maybe a minute." He dug steadily into the blackness of the lake, generating a small whirlpool at the end of each stroke. Hargreaves studied them, wondering if it would be possible to formulate the discipline of each, given all the data of course—speed of the craft, angle of entry of the blade, depth, force. Yes, it could be done. An equation could be built having all the intrinsic beauty of the whirlpool itself.

Blake was saying, "I wonder if they enjoy it. Swimming, like that."

Hargreaves thought before answering. "I guess not. I guess they just do it, like we walk."

"Walking's enjoyable," Blake said reasonably.

Hargreaves started to answer but broke off. There was something impenetrable about the back of his brother-in-law's head. It was impossible to converse, they could only exchange monologues. He glanced at his wrist watch as he stroked. Three o'clock. They should be through the portage and making camp by now. It would be dark by eight and they had the shelter to rig and food to cook. Besides which they had to find an island. At the park gate yesterday, the warden who had taken their entrance fee and given them their map of the lakes and their free trash bag had told them, "Be sure and camp on an island if you get up to Burnt Island Lake. The place is full of bears this year."

He conquered his inertia and called to Blake. "We should get on. The next portage is eight hundred yards and we have to paddle half up the lake after that."

Blake said "Aye, aye sir," and bent to the paddling, dark and crafty as he forced his paddle in and back.

Hargreaves stopped counting strokes and worked hard, keeping on course, correcting for the weather-vaning as the canoe snicked through the water into the light north-east wind. The portage was marked with the familiar yellow sign advising against smoking on the trail or abandoning camp fires without checking they were dead out. There was no beach, just a flat rock, sliding unobtrusively down into the water. Blake stepped out, a neat, sailor's movement that carried him clear of the water's edge. He held the bowline and pushed the canoe off so

it swung broadside and Hargreaves could step from the rear
seat onto the dry land. The canoe rocked as he did so and his
shoe slopped water. Blake reached out his hand, not quite
touching him, but ready for Hargreaves to grip.

"Thanks, Jim," Hargreaves said. He bent and lifted his pack
from the canoe, staggering slightly under the eighty-pound heft
of it. Then Blake did the same, grabbing it two-handed, like a
man helping a drunk.

They set down the packs and lifted the canoe well clear of the
water, clear of the access so that other canoeists could pull
ashore there without trouble. They took up their packs again;
Blake shrugged into his harness, pulling the headstrap low on
his forehead. The pack dwarfed him, but his back was firm and
he did not bother readjusting the strap. Hargreaves had a little
more trouble with his own pack, the headband would not fit
properly and he gave up on it, leaning forward instead to make
the eighty pounds dangle more comfortably from his shoulders.

Blake said, "You going to be all right?"

"Sure. The Hargreaves are part Indian, we can portage all
day." The straps were cutting already. He hoped the eight
hundred yards marked on the map was an overestimate.

They walked in single file, Blake in front, bouncing slightly
with his aggressive, healthy walk. He walks like a sailor,
Hargreaves thought—but what else could a Cornishman be?

He fiddled unceasingly with his own straps, running his
thumbs up under the bands as the weight became intolerable.
Halfway up the trail, as they crossed the rocky spine of the
watershed between the two lakes, he wanted to halt. But Blake
kept on, only the wrinkling of the top of his pack indicating
the movement of his head to follow a chipmunk and, later, a
ruffed grouse, immature and stupid, fluffing its tail at them in
the very centre of the trail.

The journey to the new lake took them twelve minutes.
Hargreaves checked the time as he brought down his wrist from
its seven or eighth trip to wipe sweat from his eyes.

Blake saw the water first and waved at it triumphantly,
Pizarro discovering another ocean.

"There's your lake," he said. He turned and sank down, a
gesture that looked like a clowning but which caused the weight

27

of his pack to be taken on a tree stump beside the trail. He eased out of the straps and stood up, shoe-button eyes bright with excitement and exertion. "This is something, this is really something," he said softly.

Hargreaves nodded, a big motion, close-mouthed, agreeable but economical of his breath. He checked his watch. It was 3:27 and the second hand was wiping away the day fast. They had very little time to find a campsite and get settled in. "O.K. Jim, now for the hard bit," he said. He slipped off his pack and worked his shoulders in luxury at the absence of weight. "Let's get our transportation up here."

"Should we sit a minute or two?" Blake asked.

He was standing, firm on his feet, shoulders well back, Hargreaves noticed. He straightened himself up the same way, feeling all the newly discovered muscles in his back taking up the strain. He wanted to sit, wanted even more to be home, in the quiet of his den among familiar comfortable things.

"Time's getting on," he said. "It'll be four by the time we're up here with the canoe, then it'll take us three quarters of an hour to reach an island." He turned away and Blake fell into step with him.

"Do you think the bears'd bother us?" he asked, his voice shining with suppressed excitement.

"They won't if we're on an island," Hargreaves said. "When you get home to England you can tell 'em we fought the bears off all night but I'd rather camp on an island."

"Me too," Blake said. "That racoon last night was enough visitors for me."

They completed the portage in a little over half an hour. In less than half an hour more they had reached an island and beached the canoe. Previous campers had left firewood cut and a stone fireplace with an old wire grille on it. Blake scouted the place and reported "luxury."

Hargreaves only nodded again. His right shoulder was aflame with tiredness and he wanted to be in his thirty-dollar Arctic sleeping bag, resting against the morning's return trip. They had left the canoe on the beach, drawn up and tied to a root. Blake did not want to camp under it again tonight. Instead he tied the rope between two trees and slung the tarpaulin sheet

Hargreaves had borrowed from the owner of the packs. It looked like a tent, nine feet long, four feet high but with open ends.

While he did it, Hargreaves lit the fire, carefully using only one fire-lighter block. The routine soothed him. His mind became a blank screen for the reception of the signals of fall in the air. He actually heard the geese approaching before Blake did and stood staring up through the pines at the watery V that complained its way across the sky.

"Must be five hundred of them," Blake said. "Think of it. Five hundred geese and not another human being in a whole day."

"Sure beats the city," Hargreaves said, and for a moment his choking feeling of Canadianness, of owning this whole place by birthright, made him almost believe his own words.

Blake said, "I don't blame them geese heading south. By looks of that sky, we could have a little weather tomorrow."

Hargreaves frowned. "The long range forecast was good, wasn't it?"

Blake cocked his head dubiously. "Could've been, but that sky'd mean wind tomorrow if this was England." His finger traced the rags of cumulus beating their way upwind overhead. "It's October; we could get a gale with a sky like that."

"I hope you're wrong, Jim," was all Hargreaves could think to say.

Later, the bush plane surprised them both. They were crouching close to the fire drinking tea while beans spluttered and simmered in their borrowed mess tins. The buzz of the plane came crowding into their consciousness and they stood up, reluctantly, to see from which direction it came. It approached out of the low sun, letting down straight towards their island, then landing and slowing as if swallowed up by its own enveloping roar. They watched without speaking as it turned, a flash of orange, and taxied towards the northern shore.

Blake had binoculars of course, a small pair of powerful German glasses which Gwen once said he had taken from a captured U-boat officer. "It's picking up a bunch of fellers in blue uniforms," he announced. "Least, it looks like uniforms, they wouldn't be here in blue suits, would they now."

"Sounds like the Provincial Police," Hargreaves said.

"Doing what, I wonder?" Blake's voice indicated that he knew, but would prefer someone with the proper authority to give him the message.

Hargreaves replied, "Looking for a missing camper I'll bet. They likely found a canoe here with no one in it."

"Well, they haven't found 'um," Blake said quietly.

"I guess they'll be back tomorrow." Hargreaves shivered. A coldness had fingered him suddenly. What was he doing here anyway? He didn't like the outdoors, except for the golf course where he played on Sundays.

Blake had not noticed the shudder. He said, "I suppose they'll keep on draggin' till they find 'um." It was another fact, like the price of bottled beer, an item of Canadian information to be stored up and retold in England at the local pub over a pint of scrumpy. The callousness bothered Hargreaves and he turned away without answering.

Later, as the darkness crept out of the water and surrounded them, they sat before the fire drinking neat rum from plastic cups, listening to the wind in the pines and the occasional heartbroken lament of a loon.

They were in their sleeping bags by eight o'clock. Blake turned over and back, then curled like a child and slept. Hargreaves took longer. He was barely warm enough even in the wind-proofed comfort of his sleeping bag. His thoughts would not rest on the island. He thought of Gwen and the children. How could they reach him if they needed him in an emergency? And he thought of the problem he was avoiding at the office. It would not go away. He had to face it. His proposal had to be ready by Monday. This was Thursday and he had done nothing. He must be home tomorrow, in time to confer with the sales manager before he made his customary run to the cottage for the weekend. How did he manage it anyway?

Hargreaves had not spent two days clear of the office in a year. This special trip to the park was his first ever, made in tribute to Gwen's brother. But his own weekend would be standard. He would work at home with his reports and his portable dictating machine. Monday morning he would hit the office at eight o'clock, having called Phyllis the previous night. By ten thirty the report would be ready for collating and by noon he would be in his car and on his way to the client. He was lying on his side, open-eyed, as he thought and he found himself smiling at a constellation he had never noticed before. Yes, this time tomorrow he would be back into the pattern of his days, his hip not chafing against a piece of basalt. He slept at last in the middle of a hypothesis.

The wind woke them at dawn, ballooning the canvas, flapping the edges with a tight, frightening crackle. Hargreaves sat up, groaning as his stiff shoulders reminded him he had been cold throughout the night. The wind, tunnelling through the length of the canvas shelter, whipped at his eyes, making them water. He gasped and wriggled backwards out of the sleeping bag.

Blake awoke instantly and crawled out after him. Unlike Hargreaves he made no sign of surprise at the wind. He stood, facing into it, hand sheltering his eyes. "Morning Peter, fresh idn't it."

Hargreaves said, "It sure is."

They walked down to the water's edge. The lake was running high, heaped into three-foot waves with white caps whipping from the crests.

Blake said, "That's blowing force six, maybe seven." His voice was just loud enough to be heard, somehow without shouting.

Hargreaves said, "It's going to be tough paddling."

Blake turned towards him, quick as a bird. "You can't go out there in a canoe."

Hargreaves felt his lips tightening, despite himself. "I've got to get back today," he said.

Blake looked into Hargreaves' face for perhaps ten seconds. "It'll blow itself out. Let's have some breakfast," he said. Hargreaves nodded. "Good thinking. I'll get the fire started." He turned away to the end of the shelter where he had stacked the kindling the night before. His temper was straining at him. How could someone with no responsibilities try to tell him what to do. He was going home today and that was that. He lit the fire quickly, using two fire-lighter blocks to promote a quick blaze.

In the meantime Blake had brought up water for the inevitable tea and he put the billy can on to boil. "What's left for breakfast?" he asked. "Did we leave any bacon?"

Hargreaves concentrated on checking the food, on keeping

31

calm. "Two packs of porridge and the rest of that peameal bacon. Two packs of dried soup, two rolls."

"Let's just have the bacon and one of the rolls now," Blake said.

"Whatever you say," Hargreaves said, knowing why Blake was economizing but keeping his voice reasonable. He fried the bacon, first cutting it thin so that it would cook quickly in the scanty heat of the fire with its flames blowing sideways from the pan.

Blake wandered away again, down to the beach to look at the canoe. He had tied it to a root the night before and Hargreaves saw him checking the knot, even though the craft was ten paces from the water.

He called when the bacon was done and Blake came trotting back. They ate in silence, solemnly splitting the dinner roll in half with a sheath knife.

When they had finished eating and were sipping their scalding cups of tea, Blake said, "I'm sorry to say it, Peter, but we shouldn't take the canoe out the way it is. Maybe by the afternoon the wind will die down."

"What if it doesn't?" Hargreaves said. "I have to get back. I've got work to do."

"Won't it wait'll Monday?" Blake asked, over the rim of his cup.

Hargreaves swallowed the last of his own tea and slashed the leaves out onto the ground. "It's got to be *done* by Monday. My meeting is Monday afternoon."

"Well, if you're stuck they'll understand, won't 'um?" Blake said. There was no pleading in his voice. He was stating facts.

Hargreaves was possessed of an urge to tell him a few facts about North America and the pressures of a salesman's life. It might be interesting for Blake to realize that not everyone moved at the speed of a Cornish villager. There were problems in business which had no equivalent in the weighing out of a pound of nails for some farmer. "It's my job," he said at last.

Blake said, "Your safety's more important than any job."

Hargreaves turned away, walking down to the edge of the water on the lee side of the island. He felt trapped, choked. There was no way of getting off this island if Blake refused. He couldn't leave the man here, no matter what he felt. He swore, letting the wind carry the words away over the uncaring water.

And then the plane passed overhead. He looked up and waved but it flew on right over the island, downwind to turn and approach, letting down towards him, perhaps a mile down the lake.

That was his answer. He could see it at once. The pilot would ring Gwen. Gwen would ring the office and tell Phyllis to assemble the information so that he could pick it up, tomorrow or possibly even Sunday. He would have to work very hard for a day but it would be done on time. He turned and ran back up the shore to Blake. "I'm going out to the plane to give him a message to phone Gwen," he called. "Are you coming?"

Blake said, "Don't do it."

Hargreaves waved a hand at him, cancelling him. "Come on, I've got to."

Blake stood looking at the ground until Hargreaves repeated, "Come on."

Then he said, "Put your life jacket on and I'll go with you."

"Great." Hargreaves bumped him on the back, jubilant. "We can stay forever once that's done."

"We may do just that," Blake replied evenly.

They pulled on their life jackets and carried the canoe down to the water. They knelt in, for greater safety and Hargreaves eased them away from the rock with his paddle. For thirty yards from the shore, while they were still sheltered by the island, they paddled true and untroubled. Then the wind leapt from behind the island and contemptuously turned them over.

The water was shockingly cold. Hargreaves screamed in alarm as his mouth, his whole head was filled with the bitterness of it. He spluttered as he bobbed up and reached for the stern of the canoe, fingers raking at the bare aluminum, scrabbling for purchase. He found it with the very tips of his fingers and dug in, seeming to buckle the bare metal as he held on. Slowly he slid his fingers over the flatness of the upturned hull and found the far side so he could draw himself to it. Only then did he think about Blake.

He spun his head around, filled with a sick horror that the man wouldn't be there. But he was, five yards from the canoe, stroking backwards, reaching out and back to grab a paddle.

Hargreaves shouted with all his might. "Come back, hang on to the canoe."

Blake shook his head, mouth tight-closed, making the last few strokes, pushing back against the force of the wind until he reached the paddle and held it firm. Hargreaves had wrenched the canoe around and was trying to paddle back towards him but the wind on the hulk was too much, he was losing ground. He rested, exhausted, eyes fixed on Blake, but the dark head over the orange life-jacket collar did not recede. It came on as Blake wielded the paddle, sitting up in the water as if he were in a submerged canoe of his own, his feet ahead of him, stroking with the paddle.

Hargreaves shouted again. "Hold out the paddle, I'll pull you in."

"I'm tied on," Blake said, his voice still not a shout even over the snapping of the wavetops flying away before him down into Hargreaves' face.

He reached down and held up the bowline of the canoe. "Round my life-jacket tie," he said.

Hargreaves could only whisper a hissing little prayer of gratitude that Blake wasn't a fool, even if he was. He looked around for his own paddle but it was nowhere in sight. He was a fool. He was a goddamn fool.

Blake was pulling himself towards the canoe, hand over hand, holding his paddle between his short strong teeth. Hargreaves felt his own way along the hull of the canoe until he could reach out to help Blake. He was stiff with cold and fear but Blake seemed quick, vital, shaking off his hand and pulling himself to the side of the canoe, pausing only to wedge his paddle down the front of his life jacket.

"Do you think the plane saw us?" Hargreaves said.

Blake did not answer. He had gone to the end of the canoe, the bow. "Get to the other end and try and right her," he called.

Hargreaves fought his way back along the hull and reached the end.

Blake called the time, a stupid call from the forties, the "two, six, hup," as they swung at the canoe. On the third

34

time they got it over, full of water but right side up. Hargreaves' teeth were chattering so hard he could hardly breathe.

Blake seemed nothing more than winded. "Do you know how to get in?"

Hargreaves shook his head. He had made enough mistakes. Let this tough little survivor take over.

Blake said, "Well, I will. You try and hold her steady." Hargreaves nodded. It was no effort to clutch the canoe with rigid arms while Blake made a monkey-like squirm over the prow of the canoe, sliding it beneath him in a quick sensuous movement. The canoe rocked but Blake lay still until Hargreaves nodded again, steady again. Then he turned over and knelt in the bottom of the canoe, in a foot of water. "Keep your feet up underneath," he called. Hargreaves only nodded, at his back this time, and lay back in the water, feet straddling the canoe, holding the stern way down as Blake paddled with machine-like steadiness towards the nearest shore. Once he tried to look up but the effort was too much and he let his eyes close again as his coldness changed to a neutral numbness that was close to sleep. The paddle blade caught him across the shoulder, jolting him with such suddenness that he wet himself in fear.

Blake's voice was rough. "Wake up, you fat useless bastard." Hargreaves spluttered, feeling anger coming up to replace the tiredness. He was not fat nor useless. Damn the man. It was all right for him, he was in the canoe. He started to speak but Blake cut him off. "Hang on and stay awake. Next time I'll knock your teeth out." That was all. Then he was turned away again, his whole body screwing down on the paddle, down and back, down and back. Hargreaves tried to count but gave up when he reached five hundred. And then Blake turned around again. "Put your feet down." Hargreaves did, and his chest filled with gratitude until he could have almost burst. Rock, slippery rock, solid beneath his feet, coming and going with the beating of the waves. "Land," he shouted.

"Tow me in," Blake ordered.

Hargreaves swung the canoe around and lurched up the rock, pulling the cold metal up and up until Blake shouted again. "That's enough, you'll hole her." Then the load lightened as Blake stepped out, waist deep himself this time and lifted the canoe, tilting it so the water gushed out and ran back, escaping back to the lake as they ran up the bank.

They did not put the canoe down until they were ten yards from the water. Then Blake dropped his paddle and began to fumble at his life jacket with stiff fingers. Hargreaves came to help him and Blake let him, standing there like a little boy as Hargreaves untied the bowline of the canoe and then the neat bows that held the life jacket. Blake slipped out of it. "Thanks Peter."

Hargreaves started to say "Thank you," but he couldn't. His voice gave way to tears and he sobbed as he turned away to fiddle with the ties on his own life jacket. Blake was prowling again, gathering an armful of dry pine twigs. Hargreaves saw him and controlled himself, squeezing his eyes shut for a second until the helpless animal sobbing had stopped. Then he began to pat over the pockets of his mackinaw, feeling for the survival pack he had let his eldest son put together for him two nights ago. A family project, one of the very very few, a joke almost, until now. He found the pack in his top pocket and drew it out. Blake was scratching together a handful of pine needles. Hargreaves knelt beside him, still not trusting himself to speak, teeth still rattling together.

Blake looked at the pack and spoke, over the tremor of his own jaw. "Good man," he said.

Together they raked up a tiny pyramid of pine needles and smashed the twigs Blake had collected. Then Blake went off for bigger pieces as Hargreaves broke out half of one of the two precious fire lighters and lit it with a wax-coated match, striking it on a rock outcropping.

The little pop of the match flame was a triumph of man's civilization. The dedicated blazing of the fire lighter was confirmation. The very sight of it relaxed Hargreaves' jaw, made him feel stronger and less afraid. He left the blaze and hunted around for more twigs, using his superior height to reach up to dead limbs that Blake had missed, not stopping until he had a bundle of wood big enough to last an hour. Then he dragged it back to the fire, enormously strong, almost proud of his previous terror.

36

Blake was crouching over the fire, warming his rigid fingers. He looked around as Hargreaves approached and began to laugh, a laugh that was too big for him, that seemed to come from the ground beneath him. Hargreaves joined in and they roared until they were weak, holding one another up, sides and faces aching, in torment from the gross relief that would not let them be. The only words Blake could choke out were "I told you, didn't I!" They laughed some more and found that they were warm, warm enough to undress and squeeze the worst of the water out of their clothes.

Hargreaves took everything off but his mackinaw and pants, spreading his shirt and underwear and socks over branches before the fire. Blake kept only his shirt and long johns on, keeping himself warm by jigging around the fire beating at his shoulders with both hands. He said, "I'm sorry about poking you with the paddle. I thought you were going to sleep."

"I was," Hargreaves said. In the part of his mind that was recovering his civilized state he wished Blake would apologize for calling him fat and useless but he knew it had been just another paddle slap, nothing personal. He felt in his pockets again for his cigarettes but they were sodden, a disgusting mess. He pulled a face and threw the bundle into the fire. "I was going to give them up anyway," he said.

Blake stopped his fire dance and said, "I've got my pipe and baccy if you'd like to share."

"Great," Hargreaves said. Then he remembered the only thing he had to offer in return. "Would you like some of my survival chocolate?"

They both laughed again until they could hardly move. And their clothes steamed, the fire spluttered and the wind blew.

Presently, as they were sharing Blake's pipe he said, "You know, I was never really worried. These lakes and woods of yours, they're kinder than the sea."

"I guess they are," Hargreaves said, but the memory of his own terror was still too strong.

Blake went on, dreamily. "Leastways you can drink the water."

Again Hargreaves could feel the chilling terror of the first mouthful of lake. He said nothing as Blake mused. "I was becalmed a day and a night once in a fog, off the Lizard. We ended up squeezing the water out of the sails. My dad and me."

"Was Gwen with you?" Hargreaves asked. It was important that she had never been that close to privation, had never chewed damp canvas to survive. That must never happen.

And as he thought it, he realized that it was the first time since falling in that he had thought of her, or of anything but his own survival. The realization made him stand taller in his steaming clothes. Nothing else would ever be quite so important.

The
Sales
Pitch

Catherine Weston laid the baby down in his crib, whisked off her apron and came back to the sitting-room for a quick clearing away of the day's toys and socks and sneakers.

"Expecting somebody?" Fred queried, over the sports page.

"Well, kind of," Catherine said.

"Who?" Suspicion pulled Fred's brush cut down closer to his eyebrows.

"Oh, you remember . . . " Catherine prodded. "The man Bert and Ellie wrote us about. How to make a little money in our spare time."

"If I didn't know you were thirty-one I'd swear you were born yesterday," Fred told her. "You can't tell a sales pitch from a weather forecast."

"They said it was a good way to make some extra money," Catherine said, patting her hair back into the shapeliness that

41

could still make Fred's heart jump to bongo time. He grabbed her by the wrist and pulled her off balance into his lap. "Hi, beautiful," he said.

"Fred, the kids are awake." She patted his cheek and stood up swiftly. At the same instant the door chimes rang.

"I'll go," Fred said.

"Well, don't be rude to the man, he's got a living to make."

"Well, he won't make it here," Fred replied. He threw the door open.

A comfortable, well-dressed man stood there smiling. He looked so much like the doctor who had delivered the baby that Fred was stunned. By the time he recovered he had owned up to being Weston and was shaking hands with the man who said his name was Jim Rudge.

"A very nice home you have here," Mr. Rudge said.

"Yeah, we like it," Fred acknowledged, backing automatically to cover up the mural perpetrated by Fred Jr.. Backing away was his second mistake. The man smiled gratefully, somehow passed him and moved into the sitting-room.

He smiled and waved at Catherine. "Hello, Mrs. Weston. I had the pleasure of talking to you on the phone."

"That's right." Catherine's smile jerked Fred back to the present.

"Look, Mr. Rudge," he said, "I'm sorry but we don't want any whatever it is, we can't afford it."

"Oh, hasn't your wife told you?" Rudge asked.

Fred bit. "Well, not exactly."

"I thought not," Mr. Rudge said. "Well, now I'm sure you know a lot of couples like yourselves. Home-owners with a young family."

"We do," Fred agreed.

"Well, my company will pay twenty-five dollars for every lead you give us."

"Where's the catch?"

"Mr. Weston"—the salesman beamed—"you're a man after my own heart."

"Oh," Fred said.

"Yes, indeed." Mr. Rudge nodded. "Nobody dictates to you, I can see that."

"Well, now, I don't know about that," Fred said. But by then it was too late. Mr. Rudge had told them that his Company, Wetta Water Inc., would install a water softener for them and enable them to pay it off by giving the names of their friends. Before Fred could take control, Rudge was in the kitchen shaking up little bottles containing their tap water and his soft water. From the start it was no contest. His samples fizzed up like a vanilla soda, while the Weston's tap water sulkily refused to lather. "And now back to our first experiment," Mr. Rudge was saying. He scooped up the two test tubes. One of them was full of a clear yellow liquid, and the other was bristling with ugly lumps of grit.

"Lemme guess which is ours," Fred said, struggling to emerge from the invisible layer of wadding around him.

"And just think," Mr. Rudge reminded Fred as he picked up the "before" tube. "Every glass of water you or your children drink is charged with about four times that much sediment."

Next, the salesman brought out a magazine rack primed with pieces about how good soft water was for the skin and the elbow joints and the kidneys.

From that moment it was all over, bar the signing—which took time. Fred found himself scrawling F. Weston after helpfully inked x's on about six sheets of paper. Then there was a flurry of equipment and magazine racks and Mr. Rudge was baring his teeth in goodbye.

"Your softener will be in tomorrow," he said, and wheeled out to the sidewalk where his shiny new automobile waited for him. Fred closed the door and sloped back to his chair.

Catherine was bending over the litter of duplicate forms Rudge had left. "Sixteen dollars a month," she said.

"It doesn't start till August and the TV will be paid for by then," Fred said.

" . . . for three years!" Catherine ended. "That's six hundred dollars."

"Nonsense," Fred said, while his own Univac meshed with the problem. Then his chin slowly dropped. "Six hundred dollars," he repeated, "and we're all signed up." He grabbed the papers from Catherine's hand and mumbled through the fine print.

43

"There must be something we can do," Catherine was saying.

"Yeah, we can pay," Fred muttered.

"But if we refuse to have the thing in the house . . . ."

"They've got us," Fred said. "They'll just dump it on the porch and garnishee my pay."

"Whatever got into us?" Catherine raged. "We could have used the money for something we needed, like a freezer or maybe air conditioning."

"Or a harmonium or mink drapes," Fred said. "Boy, is that guy Rudge a salesman or is he a salesman!"

"I won't have it in my house," Catherine exploded. "They can garnishee, they can do what they like."

Fred reached over the table and stroked her arm. "Don't worry about it, kitten," he said. "I'll ring up and cancel it, first thing in the morning."

"Can you do that?"

"Sure I can," Fred lied gamely. "Just wait and see."

The next lunchtime he was way out in the sticks, working on an overhead break in the power line. However, he borrowed the pickup and a pocketful of dimes and drove down to a phone booth on the highway. He dialled long distance and after clashing four of his dimes into the box a very superior voice said "Wetta Water Incorporated."

"I wanna talk to the sales manager," Fred said, licking his lips. After about fifteen cents worth of waiting another superior voice said "Hello."

"Oh, hello," Fred said. "My name's Weston, I don't know how to put this but we signed up for one of your machines and we can't afford it now." He licked his lips again and waited.

"Well, I'm afraid it's too late now to do anything about it, Mr. Weston," the voice said. Somehow the voice managed to make his name sound like an insult.

"How do you mean?" he queried.

"Well, the transaction is virtually completed the moment you sign the property lien," the voice said, in a let-them-eat-cake tone.

"You mean you've got a share in my house now?"

"That's the way it is, Mr. Weston." The voice had grown very fat, and the "Mr. Weston" at the end of the sentence came out suspiciously like "Mac."

"Well, is there anything I can do? I mean we can't really afford it."

"I'm quite sure the salesman didn't hold a gun to your head," the voice said.

Fred put his hand to his head ruefully, as if searching for holes. "He didn't need to. He's some salesman," he conceded. "We need that water softener like we need a grand piano."

The voice snickered politely. "Truthfully, Mr. Weston," it purred, "I'm quite sure you'll be very happy with your Wetta Water softener. And you'll find you save an enormous amount of money on soaps and detergents."

"That's all very well . . ." Fred began.

"I'm sorry, your time is up," the operator interrupted.

"And how," Fred said and clapped the receiver back on the hook. It was only then that he found he didn't have enough dimes to call Catherine. Slowly he climbed back into the pickup.

It was late when he got home.

"It's me," he called, but nobody answered. Miserably he trailed through to the kitchen. Catherine was washing the baby, who was barely visible amid great thunderclouds of lather.

"It came then," Fred said.

"It came," Catherine said, pulling out the plug and the baby in one motion.

"Pretty nice, eh?" Fred said, lifting his supper plate off the saucepan.

"The kids don't like the taste," Catherine told him. "They've just about driven next-door's crazy asking for drinks of water."

"But it's the same water," Fred quoted from the the previous night's brainwashing, "without the injurious salts."

"Well, the kids like the injurious salts," Catherine said.

Fred speared a carrot savagely.

"I picked out some names today, to send the softener people," Catherine murmured.

"I'm not going to help them," Fred said. "I'll quit smoking and we'll pay them off."

Catherine lifted her eyes from the baby and looked at Fred as if he had sprouted a pair of vivid but impractical wings. "We'll have to go along with them," she said patiently.

"We'll manage," Fred vowed, "with what I save on smoking plus the odd bit of overtime. I got an hour and a quarter tonight," he added as a clincher.

"Freddie needs new shoes." Catherine brought him back down among the earth-people.

Fred pushed his plate away and reached for his cigarettes. "Might as well finish these up."

"The list is on top of the fridge." Catherine indicated with the bottle while the baby squirmed in pursuit.

"There's only two people I hate bad enough to put on that list," Fred said, "and that's Bert and Ellie, and they've already got a water softener."

"I gave the list a lot of thought," Catherine said, in the voice she kept for use on forgotten anniversaries.

"I won't do it." Fred squandered a full inch of cigarette in one angry stamping out. "I won't set anybody up to be stabbed in the back with a water softener."

"Then you'd better find some way to bring home an extra sixteen dollars a month," Catherine told him. And that was her last word all evening. Later, Fred padded down the base-ment steps to weigh up the situation. He found the asses-milk machine sitting smug and confident under the cellar steps. It was undoubtedly in for keeps, with festoons of copper tubing around it like an Ozarks still. Fred gaped at it until his frustra-tion got the better of his common sense and he swung a vicious kick. After one blinding second his foot became numb enough to walk on and he limped back upstairs, very thoughtful.

Catherine didn't mention the list at breakfast and Fred drove off to work feeling the next best thing to good. But when he opened his lunch pail at noon, there was the letter with the list in it snarling up at him from the top of the cheese sandwiches. He jammed it into his shirt pocket alongside a roll of insulating tape. But his lunch was spoilt. Instead of chinning over the chances of the Sox in the pennant race, he sat alone in the cab of the pickup, doing some fancy thinking about what would really be best for the Westons.

On impulse, he reached into the glove compartment for a notepad. He took out the free ball-point pen the last insurance company had hooked him with and started a letter. He addressed it to the Director of Public Utilities in the town two thousand miles away where he had grown up, and began. Dear George, he wrote.

Over supper, when Catherine asked "Did you post the letter?" he was able to look her straight in the eye and say "Yes" although the letter she meant had fluttered out of the pickup's cabin in pieces on his way home. Six days went by, days filled with foamy mounds of lather. Catherine almost began to smile when she mentioned the softener. She confided in Fred that she had saved eighty-three cents on detergents that week. Except for the sixteen skins he would have to find by August, Fred found he was happy with his softener. He managed a kind of gentlemanly agreement with it. He abstained from kicking it, and it managed to dull down its gleaming newness and look a little less smug.

Then the letter came, addressed to him at work. He drove home, whistling. Pushing the door open he marched right through to the kitchen and bussed Catherine noisily on the neck. "Guess what," he commanded her.

She was losing ground to three supper saucepans and a stack of plates warming on the stove. "Give the gravy a stir," she replied, pushing a spoon into Fred's hand and darting away to retrieve the baby. Fred shouted his news at the back of her head.

"I heard from George Smith back east," he said.

"What's he got to say?" Catherine asked, whisking the spoon away from him and agitating the gravy with it.

"He needs a foreman," Fred said.

Catherine looked at him across the top of the bubbling gravy.

"Back by the sea again," she whispered.

"With the fresh air and the fishing. . . ." Fred struck out poetically.

"Would it be worth our while?" Catherine kept her voice strictly business.

"An extra twelve a week," Fred replied, lifting the lid of the pan and harpooning a potato. "Notice how soft they are in the soft water," he announced the way Madam Curie must have announced "Notice how this stuff glows in the dark."

Catherine said, "You're not fooling me. When do we start?"

Fred put both arms round her waist and swung her gaily about, scandalizing the nosy old lady across the street. "Just say the word, Boss," he told her. They finished supper, short-changed the children on their television time and put them all to bed before talking any further.

Fred was summing up the reasons, all of them good, why the clan Weston would prosper and flourish back on the native heath, when Catherine caught sight of the one snag in the plan.

"How about this place?"

"Put it up for sale," Fred said. He pulled out a stub of pencil and reached for the nearest chunk of paper. About half an inch of pencil later, he looked up and said, "We'll need to get twenty-seven hundred down to manage properly."

"For that kind of money you could get a split-level in the suburbs." Catherine gloomed. "Who's going to buy this place?"

"Another couple like us," Fred said.

"They don't come like us twice in a row. And anyway, we only put two thousand down."

Fred had hooked the phone off the wall and was dialling the number of the real-estate man who had installed them, two years before. "It's a seller's market," he quoted over his shoulder to Catherine. "Remember everybody telling us."

The second sentence the real-estate man said to him was, "Of course, you understand this is a buyer's market, Mr. Weston."

"Oh," Fred said, glad that Catherine wasn't on the line.

"I'm afraid so. However, I'll come around and give you an appraisal and put the sign up." It sounded like a chore comparable to raising the flag at Iwo Jima.

Minutes later, the real-estate man was stubbing out fifty-cents worth of cigar on the sidewalk. Then he walked slowly up to the porch and gave it a stout kick. "See how it's bellying." He showed Fred.

"I hadn't noticed," Fred admitted. In the next fifteen minutes he found there were plenty of sad little facts that he hadn't noticed about his house. The only agreement he could reach with the realtor was over his price.

"Twenty-seven's a very fair down payment," the realtor allowed, then squelched their hopes permanently by adding, "Of course, you won't find anybody with that kind of money. Gotta face facts," he said. "Anyway, I'll start the ball rolling with an ad in the *Courier* tomorrow. Watch out you don't get trampled to death in the crowds." He guffawed and left. Fred closed the door. "Just wait till tomorrow," he said, "then you'll see some action." And they did; all next day neighbours phoned to ask about the *For Sale* sign on the lawn. When Fred came home there had been only one call about the ad.

"Who called?" he asked, hooking his coat on the back of the door.

"The *Sentinel* did," Catherine told him. "They want us to put the ad with them."

"Maybe we should," Fred said.

"Let's give this one a chance first," Catherine said, ladling stew while Fred washed his hands in abundant suds. "Someone's sure to call."

While Fred was eating, the phone rang. Catherine swept up the receiver with all the poise and calm of a stockbroker during the '29 smash. "Hello." Fred watched her. "Yes, we do," she said, waggling her left foot to attract his attention. He left the table and hung over her helpfully. "Yes, right away would be fine," she said, turning to find herself enveloped by Fred's arms.

"We're as good as packed," he told her, biting her ear.

"No time for that," she said, heaving free and whisking off her apron. "Finish your supper and help me tidy round." Fred ate up and helped her. After a while he turned on the television to kill the monotony. They watched all evening and nobody knocked on their door. At ten thirty Fred wound up the alarm and prepared to hit the hay.

"They're not coming tonight," Catherine said. She peered out of the front window. Fred joined her and they both saw the big car pull up opposite the driveway. A light flicked on in it and they saw a man and woman inside enact a little pantomime of checking an address book, and peering at the front door.

49

Then the light went out and the car pulled away, like the yacht that misses the castaways in desert island movies.

"Never mind," Fred told the top of Catherine's head. "Never mind chicken, there's all day tomorrow." However, the only development next day was an outbreak of measles, two doors down. The Health Department quarantine signs looked like the kiss of death to real-estate values.

And so it came about on the second Thursday after hearing from his old school buddy, that Fred sat down to write another letter. Catherine was sitting on the other side of the room, powdering the baby's ivory-smooth bottom.

"That soft water certainly suits him" she said, carefully ignoring Fred's letter-writing.

Fred looked up from his pad, frowned and began again. *Dear George*, he wrote. *It looks as if we're going to have to pass up your offer. . . .* It wasn't right. He crumpled the page and added it to the pyramid of discards in front of him just as the doorbell rang. He reached the telephone in one bound. It buzzed uselessly in his ear and Catherine hissed "Front door!"

He sprang past her and opened the door wide. The real-estate man stood there with a pallid, middle-aged couple at his heels, like beagles.

"Evening, Mr. Weston," he said. "Mind if I show the folks through?"

"Come right in," Fred said, feeling a temptation to bow. The couple shuffled in, wiping their dry feet on the battered rug. The real-estate man began talking about the house. Fred listened in amazement. The house began to sound almost as good as it had two years ago when they came in to rubberneck before buying. The three visitors lumbered up the stairs to take in the children's rooms. Fred turned to Catherine.

"We're saved," he said.

"I'm not so sure," Catherine whispered. "That woman looks pretty crabby to me."

The three of them came noisily downstairs again, leaving the faces of the young Westons shining over the bannister. Catherine scurried up to get the children back to bed and the touring party passed through into the garden. Fred took a good look at the woman as she went by. Boy, what a grump.

50

There was a starched look about her as if her whole life was dedicated to the laundry tub, taking out her grudge on the old man's shirts. They stayed in the garden for fourteen minutes by the kitchen clock. Fred found the palms of his hands beginning to seep. Finally the door opened and the trio came back, like a delegation under a flag of truce.

The real-estate man did the talking. "Mr. and Mrs. Robinson like the house quite a bit," he said. Fred waited in silence for further crumbs of praise; he could feel the woman's eyes on him, like two gobs of soft soap sticking to his skin. "Yeah?" he prompted.

"But they're worried about this twenty-seven hundred down."

He made it sound like the National Defence estimates. He let the size of the sum crush Fred for a second then said, "They're talking two thousand." Fred felt all his little mental transistors flick on as he calculated. Seven hundred dollars less would place him squarely behind the eight ball by the time they got back east.

It was no go. The man was staring blankly at the scratches in the hardwood floor, the woman's eyes seemed to coil around Fred like pale grey serpents.

"This is a pretty nice house," he almost pleaded. "Did you see the view from Helen's window?"

"You mean the view of the park where all those children were shouting and screaming?" the woman asked sweetly.

"And the roses along the fence," Fred said. "That's the best selection on the block."

"I have hay fever," the woman disclosed.

Her husband gazed down, over his freshly-starched collar, and said nothing. Fred fixed the woman with a jinx look. Why hadn't the old biddy fallen into her own washing tub and . . . the thought came to him painlessly like divine guidance. Washing, eh. Catherine and the others watched him as he turned like a sleepwalker and moved to the kitchen sink. He pushed the tap on and picked up the soap. "Of course, this house is special in another way," he said, erecting towers of creamy lather as he washed his hands lavishly. The woman's eyes transferred from his face to a hypnotized study of the lather. Fred took a quick glance and recognized the symptoms.

Catherine had looked exactly the same way the night Water-moccasin Rudge had struck. "Yes, the lucky person who takes over here will inherit a totally mineral-free water supply," he said. The real-estate man had taken his cigar out of his mouth and Catherine was sagging her chin in wonder. Fred took fresh strength and spieled on.

"It's a boon to sufferers from various skin allergies." He rammed that jab home and it registered on the woman. She moved nearer to the sink, almost in spite of herself. Fred rinsed the suds off his hands and they stacked themselves impressively in the sink. "Clothes, of course, come cleaner, soap bills almost disappear," he quoted into the woman's left ear as she leaned over the sink. He scooped up a heaping handful of suds and presented them to her like a bowling trophy. "Ever seen suds like that?" he demanded. She shook her head dumbly and turned to her husband. He came alive long enough to croak two words: "Twenty-six." "Right," Fred said. He whipped a chair out from the table and the man sat down. Catherine mentally accepted the relay baton from Fred and vanished with the woman to study the diapers that lay Christmassy white in the closet. The happy clattering of the two women comparing laundry techniques lasted all through the signing of the "offer to purchase" which the real-estate man produced from under his arm like a .38. When it was over Fred shook the man's hand warmly and ushered them all to the door. They ambled up the path behind the dazed real-estate man, the woman still yacking about detergent hands.

Fred turned from the door into Catherine's open arms.

"You're a genius," she said.

"Of course," Fred admitted modestly. "I married you didn't I?"

They settled into the armchair for a more decisive kiss. Below them in its alcove under the stairs the asses-milk machine began to splutter and squirt as it performed its weekly self-cleansing act. Fred looked up for a moment and said, "You know, I'm gonna miss that darned softener."

Got
to
Travel
On

The three men threaded their way down the centre of the Northern Ontario Line car. The conductor came first, walking nervously, as if he wanted to look around but was afraid to. The other two men were handcuffed together, the shorter man's right wrist to the big man's left.

The prisoner paused to take a slap at one of the seats. A quick whiff of coal-smelling dust bounced out.

The cop tugged on the handcuff. "Cut the funny stuff, Fisher." He was young and tense, acting tough to cover it.

"Look at that dust." Fisher shook his head. "What a hell of a way to run a railroad."

The conductor stopped at the end of the aisle. He looked over Fisher's shoulder at the cop. "Sit in here, off'cer. Put this guy against the window."

"Good," the cop said.

He tugged the handcuff again, motioning Fisher to sit down first. Fisher did, and slid across to the window. He caught a glimpse of his reflection as he moved, and the sight pleased him. Two weeks in that one-horse jail hadn't changed him much. He was only a little paler, and the rings under his eyes just a little too dark. He wished, for a moment, that he'd been wearing his town clothes when he'd been caught. He didn't want the guys in the pen to think he was some hick in his mackinaw and his logger's boots. Still, they'd soon find out he was tough. He sat back, almost content, a solidly-built, Indian-looking bush-worker, maybe twenty-five years old.

The conductor said, "That's good, off'cer. Try to keep them handcuffs out o' sight. We don't want nobody getting scared."

They weren't used to seeing bank robbers, Fisher thought.

"Whyn't you take the cuffs off o' me," he said.

"I don't think that would be a good idea," the conductor muttered, playing with the collar of his railroad white shirt.

The cop held up his free hand and flicked a finger, elaborately relaxed. "The cuffs stay on."

"Good. That's good. I'll start lettin' the people on then." The conductor bobbed his head at the cop, then stopped himself in time from doing the same thing to Fisher, and backed away, not turning around until he was half-way up the car.

Fisher chuckled. "That's one scared little railroader."

The cop said "Just keep it quiet." But there was no threat in his tone.

Fisher looked out at the bare platform area that led back to the station shack and to the road and the endless green of the pulp bush.

"Wonder if there'll be any broads on the train," he said suddenly.

The cop said, "Don't get excited feller." And after a second's pause went on, "There's no broads worth looking at around here at all, period."

Fisher looked at him quickly, but the cop didn't meet his eyes, just sat staring indifferently ahead, beefy face working over and over his chewing gum.

"You're with the Provincials, I guess," Fisher said.

The cop didn't answer and he repeated it. The cop nodded.

56

A couple of passengers got into the coach, businessmen by the look of them, dressed a little too sharp for this end of the world, carrying flight bags. They seemed disgusted that they had to ride the train. They looked as if they travelled on airplanes most of the time. Only there wasn't any airstrip in this town, only the railroad, when the snow didn't block the lines.

There was a wait of a couple more minutes, then a girl got on. She was wearing a blue coat which she took off, uncovering a blouse made of some stuff that you could almost wrinkle up with your eyes if you looked hard enough. She was some chick, Fisher thought. She swung her coat up on the rack and as she did so she looked his way. It could have been an accident or it could have been an invitation. The cop looked dead ahead, chomping his gum. Fisher nodded at the girl, hardly a movement at all, more a thought. But he imagined he made out an answer in her look, before she sat down, midway between himself and the two salesmen up front.

Suddenly he wanted her so badly he thought he was going to pass out. His hands convulsed and the cop said, "Knock it off or I'm gonna crank the cuffs up good."

"Sorry, off'cer," Fisher said. He had to apologize, had to communicate.

"I bet you've sure seen some sights," Fisher said. "Yessir. Tell me, was you ever in a big city, the Lakehead or Toronto maybe?"

"Quit yappin'," the cop said.

Fisher sniffed as contemptuously as he dared but he shut up. No good getting on the wrong side of this guy. He could make it tough when they got out of the bush and into the jailhouse at Owen Sound. From then on, he was going to be just another con. Up here he'd been a celebrity. Hell, guys waved and wished him luck outside the jail when the trial was over. Twenty-three thousand dollars he'd have gotten away with, if that bullet hadn't nicked the back tire and sent him off the road into that tree. But down south it would be different. For the next ten years he'd be just another number, another suit of grey work clothes, making license plates in the pen.

Mother of God. He'd be making license plates for the 1984 models before he got out.

He felt his stomach flop over. Ten jeezly years. It wasn't right. He had to do *something*. He had to get away.

"I was just thinking. Nobody cares, I guess, but I get sick on trains."

"I get sick listening to you yapping," the cop said, not loudly but clearly enough that the girl in the see-through top must have heard him.

Fisher wanted to reach over with his free hand and slap that big dumb face until the tears ran. The bastard. God alone knew how long it would be before he could be with a woman again. The cop had no right to spoil it for him.

He glanced out of the window and saw the conductor walking along the platform, holding his hundred-dollar railroad watch in one hand. It must be getting colder, Fisher noticed. The man's breath was all foggy and his neck was red with the wind. He passed the window and in a minute more Fisher heard him call "Alll aboort," in the funny up-at-the-end way conductors have. And then the train was moving, pulling past the old water tower that wasn't used any more, past the station with its faded sign and on, where the bush was black green down to the very edge of the roadbed.

Fisher watched the telegraph posts start flicking by the window, faster and faster. For a second or two he was happy at the sight, happy to be moving again rather than sitting in that goddamn cell, waiting. Then the thoughts started to come. It was only eighty miles to Owen Sound. Eighty miles was less than an hour in this thing. Less than an hour and he would be passing into a paddy wagon, then an airplane, with no chance of escape, and then through the big gates of Collins Bay Penitentiary at Kingston, for ten years.

He shuddered and he thought.

If only he could escape, get off the train soon, without it stopping. That would give him twenty-four hours start. By the time they got back, with the dogs, to where they thought he'd jumped, he'd be long gone. He could slip through that bush like an Indian. Through to the lake, steal a powerboat someplace and head for one of the cottages on the islands further south. They'd be closed for the winter now, no one would visit them until the freeze-up anyway. He'd have the pick of them. And a lot of them belonged to Americans, guys with plenty of money. There was bound to be food in them and liquor maybe, and possibly even a gun. He could lie low till midwinter, saw down a gun and knock over a bank some place and get himself some real money.

It was good, thinking about the gun. A deer gun maybe, or a twelve-gauge. Something big and heavy in his hand, something that would make the broad in the teller's window at some bank go real soft at the knees, so her hands would shake when she shoved the bundle of bills over to him. Then he'd tell her to lie down on the floor, and she'd do it, real fast, and he'd walk out, nice and easy and run around the back to the car. He'd have it waiting there, running. It would be a Ford, not one of the fancy ones, a Mustang or anything dumb like that. He'd pick out a good gutsy sedan with a big motor.

For a moment it seemed to him that he was driving it now, that he was causing the trees to blur by the side of his eyes. Then his hands unclenched and his wrists thickened until the handcuffs started to hurt again.

He looked along the car. The girl was still sitting in the same place, her back to him. He stared at her head, stared hard until he thought she must feel his eyes banging up against her. But she didn't turn around.

The drab green door at the far end of the coach opened and the conductor came back, walking with tight little steps. He came up to the cop and leaned down. He had a puffy face, Fisher noticed, puffy and white like a fat girl's legs.

He said, "Everything going all right, off'cer?"

Fisher looked at him and sneered. The chicken little bastard wouldn't be asking if he didn't think that everything *was* all right and the goddamn handcuffs were sawing half-way through the wrist of the only bank robber on his train. Likely the only bank robber he'd ever seen, for that matter.

The cop said "Fine" without looking up. He made it sound flat, like he was used to travelling with bank robbers. Fisher admired him for that. He might be young but he knew where it was at, this being a cop.

The conductor sniffed and nodded a couple of times and went on, past them and out of the door and on to the next coach. Fisher felt the quick blast of cold air as the door opened and then shut again.

He looked back out of the window, moving his head quickly so that he seemed to stop the motion of a single tree for a single instant. Then it was caught up again in the green scream of the bush going by at eighty miles an hour. Fisher did a calculation, moving the facts around like pulp logs in his mind, slow and ponderous. At this speed they should be close to Crow Inlet. It was a good place for his plan. There were all kinds of fishing camps on the inlet. A lot of them were city people's places. They would be closed up now, on a Tuesday. He could get a boat without it being missed until the weekend. And by that time he could be long gone. The other good thing was that the highway swept close to the railroad track, maybe three miles away to the west. There was a long grade there on the south-bound route. The cops would likely think he'd head that way to swing up on the back of a transport. That's what a city guy would do, but he was going to fool them.

He took another slow breath, tasting and holding it like a mouthful of draft beer. He had to make his break now if he was going to make a break at all. The thought chilled him first. Then it turned to the old familiar, burning kind of fear that had ridden him in his holdup car before he got to the job.

He was going to face an armed man. His life depended on how well he handled himself in the next few minutes. If he failed, the cop would shoot him for sure.

He looked sideways at the cop again, making it a slow careful look, covering up his nervousness. The red face was still focused ahead, the lower jaw still shoving the chewing gum out and back. The sight scared Fisher, like he'd never been scared, not even when the cops were shooting at his car. This was different. He had to take this guy, from a standing start, with no gun and no club and one hand tied. Fear chilled his mouth and throat. His stomach jolted and rolled over making him feel cold, dry-mouthed sick.

Sick!

He remembered what he had said to the cop. Sick. He'd said that he got sick on trains. Now was his chance to make some-thing of it.

He jerked his free hand to his mouth and hunched his shoulders quickly a couple of times. The cop spun his head, only his head, to look at him.

"What's eating you?"

"Sick." Fisher croaked the word out. His mind was racing, high and clear up above the whole scene, looking down on the clever guy with his hand on his mouth and the big cop with the brown suit and the red ears.

"Cut the crap," the cop said, not missing a beat on his gum.

Fisher stuck to it, his shoulders still heaving, turning his head towards the window so the cop wouldn't see him stick his fingers into his mouth and force a dry, aching retch from his throat. The retching kept itself going. He was able to turn around again and make a tug at his handcuffed hand, making like he wanted both hands over his mouth. The cop didn't say anything but moved farther away until he had slipped out of his seat and pulled Fisher after him.

"Just don't barf on me," he said.

Fisher shook his head, helplessly and retched again, forcing the hard fingers down his throat again. The cop let his own arm go slack so that Fisher could cover his mouth. As they moved the three steps to the end of the coach the cop didn't stop him as he lurched through the doorway of the compartment and opened the "Hommes, Men" door.

Fisher pushed inside the tiny washroom, leaning over the toilet to retch, resting both hands on the edge. The motion was so natural that the cop didn't realize he was exposing his kidney to Fisher's elbow. Fisher jabbed him, hard and accurately. The cop gave a funny half scream and bent over. Fisher grabbed him by the throat, able to ignore the handcuff now that the cop's arms were weak with pain. He stoked up the pain some more with a knee in the crotch. And then he pressed, both sides of that thick neck, pressing deep under the ears where a guy in some beverage room had told him one time there was blood going to the brain.

It took less than half a minute.

The cop slid down to the floor, his eyes open but rolled up, like a drunk or a dead man.

Fisher threw the coat open and tugged the cop's .38 out of the holster, shoving it into his own mackinaw pocket. Then he patted the cop's pockets until he found the key ring and the tiny key that undid the cuffs. He jiggled it into his cuff and swung it open. Then, still holding the cop's hand, he passed the other side of the handcuffs around the water pipe under the sink and snapped it shut on the cop's other wrist.

His mind was still racing, cool and straight as a hawk flying.

For a start, he dropped the keys down the toilet and then flushed it, hearing a small, rushing sound as the trap opened and the keys dropped onto the track.

Then he did the smart thing.

First, he took the cop's gun out again from his pocket and hefted it, loving the slow, cold weight of it in his hands. It was a good gun, the first real pistol he'd ever handled. He took a quick glance at himself in the mirror, white-faced and determined but his hand steady and the blue-black gun looking neat and businesslike. God it was a temptation. But he wasn't dumb, like some guys. He knew what would happen if they came after him, knowing he'd taken a police gun. They'd stand off at rifle distance and drill a hole right through him. No, this was a time to use his head.

Moving quickly, he opened the chamber of the pistol and tipped the bullets down the toilet. Then he opened the cop's coat again and shoved the gun back into his holster. He snorted in triumph as he did it. Boy, would that show them guys! Didn't need a gun to do *his* work.

He patted over the policeman's pockets until he found his billfold and a small leather pouch containing six more .38 bullets. He put the billfold in his pocket and tipped the bullets down the toilet after the others.

The cop was coming round. He had started to groan and his eyes were moving.

Fisher stood up and stepped over the cop's legs which were folded up in the small space of the washroom floor. He pulled the door open an inch and looked through the crack. Nobody was around. He could see down the coach to where the girl and the men were sitting, their backs still towards him.

He thought that they would surely hear his heart pounding louder than the train as he opened the door, having to force it against the weight of the cop's legs, and stepped out into the corridor.

Quickly he opened the end door of the coach and stepped through onto the little platform. On either side of him were the steel half-doors open at the top, closed at the bottom. He opened the one on the left side of the train, the side nearest to Crow Inlet.

The wind rushed in around him, flicking the collar of his heavy coat. He licked his lips. That wind was fast. They must be moving real good.

He walked down the three little steps, pausing to read the notice in French and English warning people not to stand there when the train was in motion. Then he took hold of the rail and leaned out over the flying track, ready to jump.

The wind took his breath away, clawing at his face like an animal. He gasped and blinked but hung there until he could open his eyes properly and see where he was going to jump.

Only then did he feel frightened.

The roadbed was solid at this point, running over the bare brown Ontario rock. There was no sand, no tangles of weed, just rock.

The train passed through a low place, walled in on both sides with rock. Then it ran over an embankment, built of dead earth where no weeds grew and sloping steeply down to the jagged rocks of the natural terrain.

Fisher swore, repeating all the bad words he knew until they became a long chain, filling his mind and blocking out the agony of waiting. Then he stopped and took command of his thoughts again. He made practice jumps in his mind, trying to gauge when he would have to jump to land on a spot he had chosen.

It was then that he realized that he could not do it. Still he hung there, out in the wind, with the rock skidding by below him, but he knew he could never jump. Hell, ten years in the pen was bad, but ten years in the pen as a broken-back cripple was worse.

His face was raw cold and his eyes were filled with tears but he was sweating everywhere else. Even his hands were wet. As he hung there and hung there he kept glancing back into the train, waiting for the men to come and drag him back in and give him a chance to fight. He hoped they would not be too long about it.

All the
Care
in the
World

The bay mare was cantering in a slow circle at the end of the
lunge line. Her foal scuttered along behind her on his stilty legs,
while the lean man stood in the centre of the circle making
crisp little quarter-turns on the high heels of his cowboy boots
so that he was always facing the horses.

A stock whip dangled from his right hand but he did not
crack it. He had no cause to. Control ran out of his brain and
down his arm and along the braided lunge line directly to his
mare's head. She was an extension of himself, extra legs to puff
up the dust, extra lungs to sniff the dryness of the August afternoon. And her colt was his colt. He was man and horse and colt,
centre of the circle, circumference and tangent.

His face turned into the sunlight and out of it. The red-
painted barn, open-mouthed in the heat, gasped before him at
every turn, then the maples of the driveway, the white-painted

house and finally the paddock fence with its row of spectators. But none of it had depth for him. It was the wall surrounding his two-horse carousel, containing his world but not part of it. Someone called him from the fence; he did not look across or answer, but he moved his wrist and the horse dropped from a canter into a heavy trot, blowing hard through her nostrils. He shortened up the lunge line and she spiralled in to meet him, the foal bumping her flank as it adjusted to the new motion.

He let the whip fall carelessly from his hand and patted the mare's neck, then slapped her chest lightly, feeling for heat or dampness. She was cool and dry and he let her stand for a minute while the colt dived under her belly and bumped at her, anxiously.

Now the world was back in focus. He straightened up and rested his arm on the mare's withers as he checked along the fence to see who had been calling him.

A girl and two boys were sitting on the top rail of the fence. One of the boys slipped down and walked over to him. It was Crawford, the inevitable cigarette dangling from the fingers of his soft right hand. He came over and slapped the mare firmly on the shoulder. "She didn't fall apart on you then, Lindner." He was short and heavy and his fair hair did not suit the ragged sideburns he was growing.

Lindner said "Nope."

Crawford's eyes and nostrils were parallel black slits in the pudge of his face. He looked as if he lived on pop and hot dogs. "You coulda bin riding that mare a month anyways by now."

"Coulda bin," Lindner said indifferently. He had coiled the lunge line down to within three feet of his mare's halter. Now he stooped to retrieve his whip and then led the mare out of the paddock towards the green patch he had promised himself he would let her graze. Crawford walked with him, coughing out cigarette smoke around his words. "She's real fat, Doug. You wanna watch or she'll founder for sure." Lindner said nothing.

The youth laughed, a series of puffs around the cigarette in the centre of his mouth. Then he reached out to slap the mare under the barrel. "Look at that gut on her."

Lindner did not look around. "Ever seen the gut on you, Crawford, and you didn't have no foal seven weeks back."

66

"Ha ha," Crawford said. "Ha ha."

The girl swung the gate open for them and Lindner nodded his thanks. She was pale and pretty, a city girl of eighteen or so.

"When are you going to work her, Doug?" It seemed important.

"I guess tomorrow I'll take her around the paddock a while." Lindner paused to let his mare dip her head to the grass. "She's plenty ready."

The foal straddled its front legs and took a quick nip at the grass, then gave up in disgust and burrowed again under its mother. "There's why I don't figure on working her too hard," Lindner said softly. The girl looked at him with something like awe but Crawford snickered. "Hell, the cossacks in Russia, they milk the mares to make booze and ride the living bejesus out of them the same time."

"You some kind of Commie?" Lindner asked and the girl widened her eyes and turned down the corners of her mouth in approval of his joke.

"Smartass," Crawford said.

The girl said,"D'you think she'll be ready for the show on the thirtieth?" Lindner nodded first, before Crawford could say anything. "Might," he said. Then he tapped the foal lightly on the rump. "But this guy won't be."

The foal darted from his hand, around the other side of his mother and stood looking at Lindner, teetering on his tiny hoofs like a girl in her first pair of high heels.

The girl came over to the foal. She was tall and slender, wearing jodhpurs and a blouse you could almost see through. She reached for the foal but he skipped back and she laughed and gave up. "He's cute. What are you going to call him?"

Crawford said, "Hey, I gotta great name for it." He beamed until he had their full attention, then popped the word out. "Bastard."

The girl gasped, half laughing. "Oh, Jimmy, you're awful."

Crawford spread his arms, using the extension of his right hand as an excuse to jar the ash from his cigarette. "Why not. Nobody here knows who his father was."

Lindner did not smile. He stood, one hand on the lunge line, the other holding the whip, gazing at the foal with calm eyes.

67

"I'd say his daddy was a good part Arab. Look at the barrel on that young feller. Look at his head."

The girl said, "You're right. I never noticed, but you're right."

Crawford spat tight-lipped, like a trumpet player reaching for a high note. "Maybe his father was President Nasser for Chrissakes."

Lindner looked up at him, almost sleepily. "When you're all through poor-mouthing my horse, whyn't you take your three bucks up to Mister Dalziel and *rent* yourself a horse for an hour."

"Call them horses, that bunch of catsmeat?" Crawford tried his laugh again but it was thinner and harder than before and he abandoned it. "I got better things to do with my money."

Lindner ignored him. He had found a burr in Tuesday's mane and was picking at it with finger and thumb. He did not look up when Crawford muttered a closing comment about being able to buy a mickey for three dollars. His mind was full of the closeness of his horse, the silken warmth of her coat and the rich cakey smell of her, a smell that reminded him of breathing. The girl was still there, closer than before so that he could smell the perfume she was wearing, faint, like flowers only sadder.

She said, "What will you call him?"

He got the burr out, a round, rough bundle of points from some wild burdock plant gone to seed too early in the dryness of the last few weeks. He rolled it around in his fingers for a moment, testing the toughness of the points. Then he flicked it away and picked out the final couple of seeds from the mare's mane. "I been thinking."

He looked up at the girl, slowly, noticing the blouse and the careless charm of her hair. She was looking at him with an intentness that would have been uncomfortable anywhere else than here in the field, with his horse on the end of the rolled lunge line. She was looking for something more than words, he guessed. "I been thinking. He came out of Tuesday, I guess you could say he came after Tuesday. So I figure I should call him Wednesday." The girl laughed, a quick flutter of happiness, like a bird song. She tore up a handful of green grass and held it out to the foal. "Come on Wednesday." The foal ignored her and Lindner smiled again, without speaking. It was his foal, his and Tuesday's, and he was proud of its independence.

A car came up from the road, towing a plume of dust. It slowed at the gateway and turned in, the dust catching up and washing over it so that it disappeared for a moment. Lindner said "It's your mother."

The girl straightened up. "Oh darn. I was going to make friends with Wednesday. I guess I have to go home."

She turned to look at Lindner, look into the depths of him, her head crooked a fraction towards her right shoulder, hair swinging to the right, her eyes green as a frost sky. "Tomorrow," he said and the word was a present, something she could take away and unwrap in solitude after her mother had chewed all the goodness out of the memory of today.

"When will you be here?" she asked him, ignoring the impatient peep-peeping from the car.

"Eight o'clock. You?"

"After church—maybe eleven."

"See you."

"See you." She turned and ran to the car and Lindner had the feeling that she had not left the magic circle of himself and the mare and foal, she had widened it.

He waved once as the car backed around and sang away down the drive in low gear and erupted onto the roadway. Then he shortened up on his mare's lunge line and walked her in to her stall.

Her unshod hooves clunked on the concrete aisle between the two rows of box stalls and the foal clicked behind her, with a noise that made you think of cutting your nails.

She walked into her stall and Lindner uncoupled the lunge line and tossed it into the aisle outside the door. Then he took up the curry comb and brush from beside Tuesday's water bucket and prepared for the pleasure of working over and over her gleaming coat. There was water in the bucket but he did not let her drink; she was still a degree or two warmer in the chest than on her back so he removed the bucket for a minute or two. She bent her head to the leaf of hay he had thrown in earlier, tensing the long muscles of her neck then relaxing as she straightened again to chomp the hay, looking around at him

69

with mild eyes. Lindner began working over her coat, working
the curry comb in circles until the light dust she had picked up
during her exercise worked to the top of her coat to be brushed
away. He whistled as he worked, a mindless, minor key variation
on a popular song. After a minute or two he lifted the water
bucket back into the stall but the mare did not drink and he
felt relieved. She must be getting enough water even when he
wasn't there to check. It figured of course; Mr. Dalziel took
good care of the horses.

The foal butted against him impatiently and he gave it a
couple of strokes of the brush before it frisked away from him to
the far side of its mother. He said, "You stick around me, young
feller and you'll get to look sharp, like your momma," but he
said it quietly so Crawford wouldn't sneak in and hear him and
go around mimicking him. He didn't like Crawford, not one
little bit. It was a shame really. They could have been buddies.
Crawford was young, of course, only eighteen. But he worked in
the same kind of job, helping on a truck. Crawford was always
trying to be big though. Smoking all the time and getting Art
Johnson to buy mickeys of rye for him. And he didn't have a
horse, didn't even like riding all that much. He just liked hanging around the stable because there were girls there and once in
a while he'd get to fool around with them a bit. Like today,
saying he ought to call the foal "bastard." That wasn't smart,
just made him look dumber than he really was.

The thoughts followed one another slowly and comfortably
around his mind keeping pace with the slow circles of the curry
comb as he cared for her.

Time passed.

The quality of the light changed at the mouth of the barn,
from white to amber as the afternoon lengthened out and the
sun reached farther along the barn floor. And at last Lindner
was finished. He stood back and looked over his horse with deep
satisfaction. She was fit for the Royal, gleaming, the light chang-
ing colour as it ranged over the bulges and hollows of her flanks.
He made one last check, lifting each hoof in turn to examine
the frog for stones or bruises. She was fine. He stroked her neck
once more and then frowned. She was not perfect. He had still
not fixed the strap on her halter. The thread under the buckle

was coming unravelled. It should be fastened with a rivet. Moving slowly he unclipped the buckle and dropped the halter. The mare shook her head once or twice, trying out her bare-faced freedom, then lowered her head again to the remains of her hay. Lindner said, "I'll be back soon, momma. You shouldn't be around without a halter. You could slip down or something."

At last he picked up his brushes and the halter and walked out of the barn, looking for Mr. Dalziel and the chance to borrow a hammer and a rivet. He looked back from the door one last time. His were the only horses in the barn; the others were probably all away at the show or out on the big Saturday trail ride. Right now this was his barn.

He walked out and across the centre of the barnyard, squinting a little at the sunlight, past the paddock and out to the drive shed where Mr. Dalziel kept his tools and some odds and ends of wire and harness. Somewhere amongst them there was bound to be a copper rivet. Otherwise he would take the halter away with him and sew it.

Out of the corner of his eye he caught a glint of light, yellow against the purple darkness inside the mow of the barn. He swivelled around for a closer look but the glint had gone. It was not a flame, which was all that concerned him. It could have been a cat's eyes.

He reached the drive shed and began a slow, pleasurable search for a rivet. He dug with his fingers through the flat seed-box full of nuts and bolts and odd pieces of metal that Mr. Dalziel kept on the old, oil-stained bench. Out on the edges of his consciousness there was a cheerful murmur of birds and the occasional snicker of a horse in the top field. Beneath his hand was the satisfying roughness of the metal and in his nostrils the tingle of brass smells and gasoline fumes and the needle sharpness of new hay stored in the barn close by. Lindner was happy, a sweet, suspended happiness like that of an unborn baby. It would end in an hour or two, when dark came down, driving him away from his horse and back to the city.

He had not found a rivet. It was not important. Soon Mr. Dalziel would come down from the house to feed the horses their oats. They would work together for an hour or so, talking

horses, comparing the coats and the conditions and the appe-
tites of all the horses in both barns. Then Lindner would come
out of the barn and lean on the fender of his car for a time,
while the sky turned first pink, then red and then purple.

The glint caught his eye again. This time he tracked it and
held it. It was a bottle, flat and golden. A whisky bottle, and
Crawford was using it like a mirror, flashing it to attract his
attention. As he looked up Crawford called to him. "Hey Doug.
C'mere."

Lindner walked up the bridge of the barn and through the
open door. On either side of him, the bales of hay and straw
reached to the roof. Only the centre was free, the floor littered
with loose straw, a couple of the square bales set flat for seats.
Crawford was straddling one of them, the mickey of rye swinging from his right hand. "Have a drink, buddy. You bin
working." There was about half a bottle left. And Crawford
was swaying.

Lindner said, "You drunk all that by yourself."

"Sure thing. Little snort's good for a feller."

"You'll get sick," Lindner said.

Crawford laughed, rocking back and forwards until he almost
toppled from his bale. "I'll be sicker if'n I finish it all up. Take
a slug." He thrust the bottle out, so violently that a small jet
of it jolted from the open neck. Lindner took it. "You know I
don't drink."

Crawford clapped his hands, once, rocking back on his hay
bale until his feet were clear of the ground. "Right. Right.
You're the guy who doesn't drink, doesn't smoke, doesn't screw
around. I forgot." He shook his head, hugely, as if playing to a
big audience. "Tell me, Dougie baby, what *do* you do for fun.
C'mon now." He beckoned with both hands, rocking back
again, then leaning forward in mimed laughter.

"You're too young to drink. Gimme the cap." Lindner held
out his other hand but Crawford only shook a finger at him.
"Too late, man. I threw it away."

"Why'd you do a thing like that for?"

"So's we could finish the bottle. What the hell, it's only a
mickey. Can't get far on that." He had ceased clowning now, his
movements becoming more imprecise, his eyes owlish. Lindner

judged he had drunk most of the whisky in one belt and was just beginning to feel it.

"You better go easy. I'll keep a hold of this," he said.

"You will like hell." Crawford stood up, took one swooping stupid step and reeled back against the wall of hay behind him. "Gimme my bottle." He held out his rubbery arm. Lindner dropped the bottle to his side, holding it loosely by the neck. "You can't have it. You're too young to drink. You could get Mr. Dalziel in a whole lot of trouble if the police came up here."

Crawford made an obscene gesture. "Mr. Dalziel can go . . . ."

"He's a nice man. I don't wanna see him getting any trouble over any cheap drunk," Lindner said. He discovered he was enjoying himself a little. He was glad to see Crawford couldn't handle whisky.

Crawford sat down again on his bale, mustering all his control. "Just because he owns a farm an' a buncha goddamn horses he's Jesus Christ to you. You know something Doug? You're a nice feller yourself, but you're awful dumb. You know that?"

He reached into his pockets, slowly and deliberately, as if his only purpose was to warm his hands. And then before Lindner could bring himself to believe what he saw, he had taken out a cigarette and was lighting a match. Lindner dropped the bottle and snatched at the cigarette. "Not in the barn. You're not that drunk. You can't smoke in here." Crawford gazed at him, dull-eyed. "Hey," he said, "what'd you do with my cigarette?" But like a robot programmed to complete his action, his hands swept past one another and the match popped into light.

"Blow it out!" Lindner snapped, but Crawford only laughed, craftily and turned away from him, cupping the flame into his hands. "Screw you," he said.

Lindner hit him, too hard.

He meant only to slap his face to smarten him up, but Crawford was off balance so that Lindner struck him with the heel of his hand instead of the fingers, struck him on the temple instead of the cheek. Crawford collapsed, and the match dropped with him, and the match book, erupting into a flame that spread a yard wide as it hit the straw-covered floor.

Lindner threw himself down on it, beating the flame all but out. Only the corner eluded him, snatching upwards to the corner of the nearest bale and the one above it and the one above that, transmuting the tender gold of straw into anger. Lindner stood on tiptoe, smashing at the flame with the halter he carried. The flame escaped him, climbing higher, spreading sideways, singeing the loose faces of the bales, preparing for the deeper bite that could never be cancelled.

Lindner kicked at Crawford. "Get up. Get up. You've started a fire." He screamed it as he slashed at the flames with his halter. "Get water. Quick." Crawford only groaned and rolled up onto his hands and knees like a good uncle playing horsie.

Lindner ran out of the barn, heading for the water trough. He shouted as he ran but he was aware that no one was listening.

He reached the trough and scooped out a pail of water, knowing it was too little and too late but not sure what else to do. He ran back with it to the barn but the flames were beyond his power to douse them. Already the heat made him duck back as he entered the barn and the first puny cracklings had become a steady hissing roar of heat. He slapped his bucket of water up at the face of the blaze and was rewarded for one moment by seeing a patch of black break through the face of the flames only to be lost again before he could turn back for more water. His eyes were smarting from the heat and the white, ghastly smoke that was filling the barn but he could make out Crawford, still on hands and knees on the floor. He dropped the bucket and grabbed Crawford by the collar, swearing at him in a terrible scream.

Crawford was weeping and trying to walk but his movements were too slow to be useful and Lindner had to haul him clear. He dragged him to the door and pitched him head first down the bridge of the barn on to the short green grass at the foot. He turned to duck back for his pail but already the heat was too intense. His face was seared and his eyes could not accommodate the brightness. His heart pounding, he turned and ran once more to the water trough. Now there was no pail.

He stood for a second, undecided, knowing he should be acting now to reach his horse in time but committed to acts of appeasement for his guilt and shame at his own part in causing the fire. Should he look for a pail? Help Crawford who was blundering around, sick drunk? Or should he run to the house to alert Mr. Dalziel. And would that be the best thing?

Angrily he turned and ran to the house, and as he reached the door almost collided with Clyde Dalziel who was running out to the barn, white -faced and shouting, "Get buckets. For Chrissakes get buckets." Together they pounded back to the drive shed where Dalziel snatched up a couple of battered buckets from under the bench. "Quick, get some water in there." He was screaming, as if the growing heat from the barn were drowning his ears in sound.

Together they dug their buckets into the water trough and Lindner felt the rim of his bucket strike the bottom of the trough and knew there was not enough water in it. There could never be enough.

The heat from the mouth of the barn was too fierce to allow them even close. They slashed their pathetic buckets of water from the doorway, then ran back for more. Crawford was alert now, running after them with another bucket, shouting. Lindner heard the words as sound, part of the formless roaring of the incandescent moment. They made no sense even when his mind sorted them and fed them to his consciousness one at a time. "Lindner . . . did . . . it . . . made . . . me . . . drop . . . the . . . matches. . . ."

He recognized Dalziel's bitter snarl as the three of them baled more water from the dropping level in the trough. "Stupid bastards."

Before they even reached the barn, Lindner knew it was too late. The mow was a single block of fire. Fire defined each vertical board of the barn's frame in a line of orange light, drawing its own substance from the air about the barn, darkening the flat, afternoon light. The doorway was a waterfall of sparks rushing inwards in a solid curve. Dalziel shouted, "It's no good. It's too late."

Crawford repeated the same words as before, "Lindner made me drop the matches," as if it were a magic spell that would put out the fire. It was at that moment, as his dried lips searched for an answer that Lindner gave up trying to make amends. He dropped the bucket and ran down the bridge of the barn and to the side door. It was cooler against the closed wall of the barn but as he reached the doorway the heat lashed back at him. Fire was there before him, smoke and heat pouring from the open doorway. He covered his face with his forearms and ran up the aisle towards the plunging, terrified form of his horse. Above him the floor of the mow was burnt open, he was standing at the base of a chimney and he knew the walls were only straw and would collapse in a few seconds more burning.

He flung the door of the box stall open and reached for his horse's head. The foal came between him and the mare, whinnying high and thin. He pulled the foal aside and grabbed again for the mare's head but there was no halter to hang on to. His hands slid uselessly down her neck as she reared, striking out in terror with her front feet.

Without thinking of the pain he tore off his shirt to throw over her head but it was singed and brittle and it split as soon as he put it over her. The heat seared him, making him cry out with pain. He tried for one last second to loop the shirt over her neck and pull her head down but she reared again, shredding the shirt, swinging him against the hot iron of the stall door. With the tears boiling in his eyes he let go of the shirt and seized the foal, half carrying, half dragging it into the open. Behind him the screaming of the mare grew more shrill as she plunged about between the walls, tortured, blinded, and now bereaved.

A sudden rush of blazing straw descended between her and Lindner as he reached the door. There were people all around outside, shouting things, and someone tried to hold him and wrap a blanket around his shoulders. Frantically he tore the blanket off his shoulders and tried to go back in. But the heat was a wall now, with a substance no flesh could break through. "My horse is in there." He thought he was shouting but the words did not seem to have any sound. Then more people were clawing at him. And through the yellow fantasy of the flame he could see his horse, her coat whitened with burnt hair, screaming and twisting. And then Dalziel was beside him with a rifle. Lindner watched him, not even sure what was going on as Dalziel raised the gun and aimed. Only then did Lindner know what he alone had to do. "Give it to me," he shouted and this time the words were all aloud.

As he seized the rifle it fired and Dalziel shouted an obscenity that whined away in the same timeless dimension filled with heat and fear that had swallowed up the bullet.

Lindner put the gun to his shoulder, wincing despite himself from the pain of his blistered flesh. Tears could not exist in the heat from the barn but his muscles were weeping as he pulled the trigger, and as fast as he could work the bolt sent round after loving round into the big mare.

Bed and Breakfast

With the cunning of a man much older than twenty-one, James Lucas Jr. made her drink a solid double. His own would have been illegally weak if served in a bar. No sense taking chances with this opportunity. He left the kitchen and returned to the party, breathlessly.

Anne Granger mouthed a shallow smile and gulped her drink. James watched her cautiously. With any luck she would be the first of many girls to share his new bachelor apartment. She gazed back at him over her glass and he frowned with the intensity of finding something progressive to say. She said it for him.

"You have a headache."

"No"—he hedged craftily—"but this place is getting awful rowdy."

"Why don't we leave?" she asked, and he spluttered in his ice water. Really, for a woman of thirty-plus, she was frighteningly naïve.

"I know just the spot to go," he said hoarsely. "It's quiet, and we can have a drink."

"I hope it's not too far," Anne yawned, baring her slightly pointed teeth. "I still have to find somewhere to stay."

James Lucas forcibly swallowed his Adam's apple. The elaborate conversational trap he was preparing swayed and collapsed. He abandoned all pretence. "Leave it to me," he said.

Within seconds they were speeding down Avenue Road in a taxi. Within minutes they were opening the door of his paint-perfumed bachelor apartment.

"Nice," she said, slipping out of her coat.

"I like it," James said modestly, kicking a pair of dirty socks under the bed. He felt as though he were taking oxygen. His plan was working like witchcraft. He stepped into the next phase.

"How about Scotch?"

"Fine," she said, and then cut the ground from under his feet with—"but not dynamite like that last one."

The back of his neck was towards her, and he could feel it glowing with shame. With disarming familiarity she moved to the record player and clicked it on.

"You men have all the luck," she said, snapping her fingers absently to the Latin American music.

James was mentally agreeing and he remained silent. She took the drink and curled on the couch, carelessly letting her dress ruckle over her knee. James began to draw short breaths.

"I suppose you know I've got a family," she said. "Or haven't you been at the agency long enough to learn all the scandals?"

James lifted his eyes to her face. "I had heard," he mumbled. This was to be the pay-off, he supposed. Get him walking on cloud nine and then drop him in his tracks with talk of the devoted husband and fair-haired sons. It was going to hurt. She looked at him and giggled.

"Don't worry, dear, I'm not going to get all moral on you." An intangible pegboard formed inside James' head. Mentally he reached up and pegged his first score. She smiled at him again, the way she had done at the party. "It's just that I envy you your freedom." She waved the hand that held the glass. "I'm separated from my husband, but am I free?" James watched the dizzy swirling of the drink with new alertness. What could she say that would come between him and the half-promise she had just made him?

"Of course I'm not free." She beat in upon his silence. "I'm living with my mother and two kids twenty miles from town. Whenever there's a party I'm stuck with a last bus to catch, or a hotel bill." Before James could phrase his Ideal Solution, she added, "What I need is a snug little *pied-à-terre* here in town."

James found that his vocabulary had failed him in his hour of need. He set down his drink and advanced purposefully. They kissed, a long, exploring kind of kiss. Anne drew back her head to nose-rubbing distance and said, "Wow, you're quite a boy!" Thirty-seven minutes later James Lucas was in a deep, well-earned sleep.

Life flowed back into him next morning with a peculiar intensity. His ego was the first part of him to wake. It seemed too big for him, cramping awkwardly within his buzzing head and relaxed limbs. As memory returned he began to smile, awarding himself ten out of ten for a brilliant campaign, skilfully carried to its end. He sat up and became aware that he was still undressed, and was alone on the couch. The only evidence of his conquest was the rushing of the shower and a pair of high heels lying within kicking-off distance. He smiled a lazy smile and fished for his crumpled cigarettes. The bed was enticingly rumpled. So she had slept there alone. Well, never mind, she had earned it. He inhaled his cigarette smoke deeply. He was launched on the exciting, the richly rewarding life. No more gymnastic tactics in parked cars. No more risk of embarrassment in lovers' lanes that suddenly filled with people. James Lucas was a man about town, no ties, no obstacles, no regrets.

The shower stopped and he rose abruptly and rattled the bathroom door. It was locked.

"Just a minute." There was shyness in her voice, he decided. He turned and surveyed his reflection in the glass of his graduation photo. After all, the poor girl was hopelessly . . . what was the word? . . . compromised. He smirked again, backed away from the door, and began to dress. After a pause which honed

his nerves to an unexpected jumpiness, the door opened. She
did not look at him, but walked directly to her shoes. He
strolled across to her, swinging his legs in his new, boulevardier
manner.

"Hi," he said, chucking her under the chin.

She smiled briefly. "Hi," she said.

What was going on behind that impassive expression? he
wondered.

"Is there anything in the fridge?" she asked.

"Sure, there's all kinds of goodies," he said, holding her hands.
"We can eat later."

"I have to catch a bus." Her regret warmed him. "I'll get some
breakfast while you freshen up." With a wifely motion she spun
him around and pushed him towards the bathroom. He shrugged extravagantly and moved away. After all, he'd had his fun.
It wouldn't hurt to be a little gallant to the victim of his conquest, the first of many.

He showered and shaved, whistling loudly the whole time.
Except for a tinge of blueness about the eyes, he was looking his
best, he decided. Promiscuity certainly agreed with him. He
combed his hair and opened the door.

A revitalizing smell of frying bacon led him by the nostrils. In
the kitchen he found Anne expertly flipping food onto two
plates. Coffee was simmering agreeably on the stove. He stood
behind her, put both arms round her waist and kissed her on the
side of the head. She stopped working for a single moment, and
then proceeded with cutting the bread.

"Any regrets?" he asked. It seemed such a sophisticated question.

Flatteringly she stopped and turned to him. "Not a one,"
she said soberly. He smiled a worldly smile he had been practising while he shaved.

"I'm glad," he said.

She turned away and picked up the plates. "I hope you like
your eggs over."

"Anyway you do 'em is fine with me," said James. Women
were strange . . . he had always thought there would be regrets
and possibly tears. But here was the adult approach: the party's

over, let's part friends and go our separate ways. Pensively he reached for the salt.

Anne poured coffee and brought him the cream. There was no doubt his attentions had gratified her. After all, she was a little long in the tooth. Probably not many guys would have given her the benefit of their company. But a young man had to start somewhere.

They finished their breakfast in silence. With the food came a return to a more routine line of thought. He must get her out of here quietly, and finally. She stood up at last and he brought her coat. She sensuously slid her arms into the sleeves and he swallowed hard. Suddenly she turned and put both her arms around his neck. "You've been so kind," she said.

"It's been fun." He smiled graciously. But it was all over. On Wednesday, there was the annual Art Studio party at Phil's. It would be a cinch to find a girl, one of the lush young models maybe.

"I'll be staying in town again on Wednesday," she was saying. "There's a party I've been asked to."

"Oh?" was all he could muster.

"At Phil Warden's." She confirmed his growing anxiety. "How would it be if you came along? It should be a load of fun."

"I've been invited already," he said.

"Fine." She patted his cheek. "I'll see you there, and we can get together again later on."

"I'd like that," he said, through dry lips.

"So shall I," she said, in a suddenly businesslike tone. "And while I think of it, get in some more bacon. Oh, and I like Branston pickles with my breakfasts—better get a large jar." She reached up again to pat his cheek before leaving, and it seemed to James that a hook sank into his flesh.

A
Present
for
Alice

Wright took the eighteen dollars, not looking at the clerk. He counted the money and folded it over and over in his truck-driver's hands until the five bills took on an illusory thickness. Then he nodded towards the wicket and walked out, past the mouthy old commissionaire with his First-World-War ribbons.

The street felt good after the marble and whispers of the unemployment office and he wriggled his shoulders, filled with sudden, useless vigour. A truck was loading at one of the cut-rate furniture stores and he ached to help, to lift and grunt and feel his stomach knit up tight over some honest-to-god work. But the men didn't need help, they were working fast and clean, the way he would have worked. He spat into the gutter and walked east towards the apartment.

A barbershop calendar caught his eye. He stopped, frowning. Somebody ought to tell the guy that drew the picture that women weren't shaped that way, leastways, Alice wasn't. He dropped his eyes from the blind, impudent smile to the date—April 18. Yes, tomorrow would be their anniversary. And he couldn't even afford a lousy card for Alice. He noticed the barber's face mirroring his own through the glass, mouth curved in the patronising smirk of the man who owns dirty pictures. Wright sniffed and turned away.

His hand had begun to sweat and he slackened his grip on the bills. Eighteen dollars! By living on fresh air and not smoking or buying Alice even a lousy card for their anniversary they would end up the week another four or five bucks in the hole. What a wonderful way to celebrate ten years of being married. He sniffed again and raised his head, taking a long look at the street he was walking, seeing it the way an immigrant might see it, the way his old man saw it thirty-eight years ago when he landed from Liverpool. The land of opportunity—boy, that was funny. Some opportunity! The opportunity to quit school at fourteen so you could pull down fifteen bucks a week delivering coffee. The thin, spring sunlight chilled him. He shivered and walked a little faster, back towards the apartment with its endless TV shows and the kids yelling, and Alice . . . Alice. Well, that was one good thing in his life, he had to admit that. Here, they'd been married ten years, and all the sweet talk and all the promises he'd made, he meant all of them. Nobody figured it would work out between them, her the high school kid, and him the delivery boy. But it had worked out. They had a nice little family and he still loved her just as much and all that. He scratched his chin, like a man caught perjuring himself in the witness stand. All right, so he wasn't telling all the truth. The other promises hadn't turned out so grand. No house, no car, no none of those things they'd planned on. But Alice hadn't bitched. Not *bitched*. Sure she was getting kind of tired of having him around the house day after day, but who wouldn't?

Slowly, like the last traces of an anaesthetic, his reverie dispersed, leaving him vividly aware of his surroundings. He was directly in front of a newly painted store. The windows were blanked over with signs reading "Auctions ten times daily," "Free Gifts. No minimum, no reserve." The sound of the PA speaker over the doorway pressed downwards almost physically on his head. The door was open and the room was half-full of men standing round the raised platform where the auctioneer was holding up a gilt clock. Wright felt himself drawn, the smaller body towards the larger, to the back of the crowd. A man next to him was dragging on a handrolled cigarette and Wright could almost taste the crispness of the smoke. He swallowed quietly and looked inwards to the man on the platform.

"And where else would you see a classical timepiece like this for a mere three dollars and fifty cents. Who says four? You do? That's generous, that's real swell. A fifteen-dollar clock and he says four dollars."

The auctioneer rolled his eyes upward, shrugged, passed the clock to an assistant. The crowd laughed. The auctioneer said, "So give the gentleman one of those flashlights there. He's gonna be big, we're gonna be bigger. Yes sir, no extra charge. Four bucks only—and you get a flashlight as well."

Wright tightened his grip on the five bills and moved, as if by osmosis, to the front of the crowd. Might as well be up here, may click for one of the free gifts—a ball point pen maybe, to keep the kids quiet, maybe even something he could give Alice for a present. The auctioneer's patter dribbled on, the correct timing of jokes, praise, sneers; a disarming competence that impressed Wright, even as he saw through it. A few combs were tossed out between points in the sales pitch, but they went over his head, back towards the stragglers who were not yet part of the crowd. He began to lose his fear of the place, his right hand slackened on the thin wad of bills. And then he saw the first really valuable offering. The man pulled the electric frying pan out of its box. The aluminum glowed with a subdued, serviceable gloss, the black handle was filigreed with the white figures for settings and conditions. It was a perfect gift. The man on the platform spun the pan in his hand, like a tennis racket. "Here's an easy way to get in good with the old lady for a whole year," he said, and Wright's lips were moving with his. The auctioneer paused and waved the pan. "You'll get breakfast in bed for sure. You can do the cooking right on top of the counterpane. How about that, eh? Bacon and eggs right on the pillow. How's that sound?" He gave a definitive little shake of the head. The crowd was silent. "Who's gonna start me off, who'll put a price on this marvel of modern domestic engineering?" No one spoke. Wright's heart felt as if it were flopping around unattached in his chest. Would nobody put in a bid? Maybe he could grab the thing for two bucks. The sign said there was no minimum, no reserve. A voice strange to him muttered two, but the auctioneer was looking out over the back of the crowd pronouncing "Three." A flick of the head the other way, "Three *fifty! Thank* you sir." "Four." Wright felt a lusting, hunting rage. The dirty chiselling . . . they were cheating him out of Alice's present. They thought he was a bluffer, counted on him folding, just because he wasn't wearing the sixty-dollar suit and the two-tone shoes. "Five," he said crisply.

"Six, seven . . . eight." The auctioneer caught the bids from over Wright's head. It was the same story, Wright fumed, short guy on defence at the basket, the big guys, high rollers just lobbing their shots in above him. Well, he'd backed away too often. Now he was going through with it.

"Nine." The syllable bounced insolently off the back of his head. "Ten," he said, finally catching the auctioneer's eye. The gavel nailed his word down tight. Wright watched triumphantly as the frying pan was passed to the assistant for wrapping. He felt winded and realized he had been holding his breath all through the bidding. He relaxed with a quick, shuddering gasp. The assistant wrapped the parcel and snapped the string with a tug. "Take it easy Mac, you bought it, not won it," he said. "That's all you know, feller," Wright thought. He unfolded his slim roll and handed over the ten, snapping it between his hands. The assistant took it, nodded and turned back to the platform. Wright turned away, the long parcel held casually under his arm.

The doorway of the store stood square before him, a yellow slab of light. And as he passed through it dazzled him, illuminating suddenly the folly of what he had done. Ten dollars! He must be out of his mind.

The PA voice shattered above his head, incomprehensible as the clanking of faulty machinery. In fact that's what it was. A stinking, lousy machine that dragged guys in and flailed the sense out of them. His anger of a few moments before rose in his throat. He'd been taken. Wrapped up and taken for a ride like a country kid on his first trip to the city. He plunged back through the doorway. The auctioneer was talking, gesturing, laughing, unreal as a movie seen from behind the audience when you arrive late. Wright swallowed, his anger turning inwards upon himself. He wasn't going to do any good here, that was for sure. He edged back into the crowd and up to the assistant's side, glad that the crowd was looking up and past him to the new object on the block. The assistant was looking up, too, gum slapping over and over in his restless mouth. Wright said, very quietly, "Pardon me."

The assistant grinned, in concert with the crowd's laugh. There was a bland admiration of the auctioneer on his face, and Wright's chest grew heavy at the sight. There would be no pity here. He reached out and nudged the man's arm and the face turned towards him, mouth a vertical oval as it worked the gum. "Yeah?" Wright pushed the parcel towards him, fiddling rapidly at the knotted string. "Listen, I can't afford 'a buy this. I never meant to buy nothing. I'm on relief, for Chrissakes." The man shrugged, politely, as if Wright's words had been in some foreign language. Wright felt the heads nearest to him swing round, away from the platform. He flushed. The auctioneer raised his voice a fraction, the assistant turned back towards him. Wright said, "Mister, listen to me. I gotta get my money back. I'm out 'a work."

The assistant said nothing, only his hand moved, wrist sagging disinterestedly, pointing to the small notice over the door, where no one could see it until they had turned away from the business platform and were leaving the store. It read: "All sales final."

"But, listen 'a me. . . ." Wright stopped as the auctioneer suddenly dropped his banter and the store sank into an echoing silence. The bright little eyes turned down towards Wright. "Something not right, *sir*?" In the fractional pause that followed, Wright opened his mouth, but was drowned out by: "Not the kind of service you're used to getting from Abel's department store with six floors of clerks to serve you? Well, that's why you don't pay Abel's fancy prices in here. You buy here, you save. You get a good look at the merchandise first, you bid, you buy. That's it, eh?"

"But I'm out of a job," Wright whispered.

"How's that, friend?" The cupped hand over the ear, the stoop, the wink at the crowd.

"I'm out of work," Wright said.

"We don't hold that against you." This time there was a snicker from the crowd.

Wright pushed the parcel towards the auctioneer. "I can't afford it." He wasn't looking at the man, the whole room was out of focus, the faces whirling about him like snowflakes. He felt the parcel taken cleanly from his hands. "Sorry, sir, no credit allowed, put this back in stock, Andy," the voice was saying.

"I paid for it," Wright said. "It's mine."

"Then take it and get out o' here." Still Wright could not meet the brilliant competence of the eyes. "For ten bucks you get a forty-dollar frypan, and you complain. . . . My best friends should have such sorrow." Another laugh, washing over Wright from all sides. He clutched the parcel to him and burrowed through towards the door, stumbling across the damp softwood flooring.

The street gripped him, drawing him quickly east. He went, letting the colour of the sunlight wash every thought from his brain, seeing everything he passed with painful, new-born vividness. He crossed a street, against the light, unaware of the car that swerved and honked at him. On the far corner he stopped and his stupidity overtook him, like a messenger running after him with a forgotten umbrella.

What had he done? Spent half the money on a gadget they needed like they needed ulcers. A frying pan, for God's sakes, when they had nothing in the house to put in it and no chance of getting anything.

His misery filled every part of his body, softening his bones so that he could have collapsed from his own weight. Ten dollars! He could imagine Alice's face wrinkling up, horrified, as she mouthed the words. How to get in good with the old lady . . . that's what the man had said. Boy, if only he knew.

His feet were leading him slowly back to the worn stairs of the apartment. He stopped abruptly. Goddamn it! He was a man, master in his own home. So he'd bought a frying pan. It was a present for her. It was a nice gesture he was making. Now they'd be able to have breakfast in bed . . . if only they had anything for breakfast. And in his mind he saw again Alice's lips parting and falling silently over the words "Ten dollars." No, he couldn't face that. Not in front of the kids. He'd have to think of something.

He would sell it. Forty dollars the man had said it was worth. Well, no use fooling yourself. He was likely blowing a little. But it should be worth twenty bucks anyway. He might even make a profit. Maybe enough for a couple of steaks or a case of beer. The thin sunlight glittering on the street's store fronts became suddenly warmer. He stepped out to the edge of the sidewalk, reading the store fronts left to right like a newspaper headline: *Small Fry—Bert and Ellie—Paisan Bakery—Kovac drugs—Marcus, everything bought and sold.* Marcus. Sure, that was the guy to see. Wright pulled the parcel closer under his arm and walked quickly to the little store. He paused outside, checking. The window was a treasure-chest he had dreamed, at twelve years old, of finding open. Guitars, guns, power tools, typewriters, a trombone with the mouthpiece tarnished brown. Even now the childhood charm reached out to him, slowing him down. There must be a dozen good livings lying right there in the window. A guy could get to be a western singer, a carpenter, a band leader like Tommy Dorsey, anything, even a hunter to live off the land a thousand miles from employment offices and auction galleries. He opened the door timidly, rubbing his lower lip backwards and forwards between his teeth. Maybe the old guy would be generous with him, give him more than twenty bucks. Just as a loan, like. He'd be glad to get the pan back once he got steady work.

The door opened silently, and away down the long funnelling hall a dog barked, automatic as the ringing of a bell. Wright took the two steps into the store and set his parcel down on the smooth old counter. The bark grew louder and abruptly dwindled as an inner door was opened and closed. Marcus came forward between his tight-pressing walls of abandoned treasure. Wright looked down slightly into the tiny old face. "Hi, Mis' Marcus."

"Good day." The old man turned away from him, hands

fluttering at a record player that had slid too far into the aisle. Wright spoke at the back of his head. "I got something you might like to buy, something good."

"Buying, buying. Nobody ever made money buying. I got everything I need. I should sell, every day for a coupla months maybe."

Wright ignored the old, old, buyer's voice. You had to be sharp to deal with these guys. He wasn't going 'a get sucked in another time today. "Wait'll you see it," he said.

The old man found other spidery little chores for his eyes and fingers while Wright untied the parcel and laid the frying pan on the counter. "How's about that?" he asked hollowly.

Now, at last, the old eyes swivelled up towards his own. *"This?"*

"Well, sure." Wright swallowed. It didn't have to be twenty, just ten would be fine. Just ten.

The old hands flicked close to the pan, not touching. "Such a make who ever heard of?"

He was interested! Wright's hopes revived.

"Good make. The company makes under license to one of the big companies in the States," He felt his face tingling with anxiety.

"And for this you are no doubt looking for big price, ten dollars maybe."

"Twenty," Wright said quietly.

"Good day, Mister." Marcus turned back down the corridor.

"Jussaminute!" Wright reached for the old man's arm. The fabric of the sleeve was abrasive between his fingers. The old man shrugged himself clear, eyebrows descending angrily.

"Par'n me, Mister Marcus." Wright licked his lips, easing the defeated words up out of his chest. "I just bought it. I got sucked in at the auction up 'a street. I'm out 'o work, I gotta sell it."

Now Marcus moved back to the counter, contemptuous thin fingers turning the pan over, monkey knuckles rapping on the bottom. "So I should pay for your mistakes, maybe?"

"All I want is a few bucks, just'll I get a job." Wright rested his finger tips on the counter, pressing down to stop himself grabbing at the frying pan to rescue it from the old man's contempt.

"I give you three dollars." The words clattered, hard as coins at Wright's feet.

"Three bucks? You must be fooling. I paid ten for that pan, not five minutes ago."

"Then you need someone should examine your head." The old man's mouth moved with his fingers as he flicked at the lead, rapped the metal, twisted the handle. But the words didn't reach Wright. Instead, a soundless roaring filled his ears. Had he really been that much of a fool? Ten bucks worth of milk out of the children's mouths just so some smooth talker could smoke thick cigars and take fancy broads to the Towne Tavern. His eyes prickled with furious tears and he jammed his lips tight together, repeating all the dirty words he could think of over and over in his head. He reached for the pan and wrapped it. A single sliver of his mind itched for Marcus to reach out and take the pan from him. But the biggest, most hurt part of him was glad when the dealer shrugged again, hands uppermost like some Hindu image, and moved back down the hall towards the metronomic barking of the hidden dog.

The wind was clean on Wright's face when he reached the street. It carried the surprising warmth of the waterfront mud on it; the singing wet-feet-and-rafts smell of long ago before Alice Kowalski had let him, that night under the willows. The sidewalk passed beneath him, carrying store fronts and white faces at windows and setting them up behind him to jeer at his bent back. He would have to take it home now. Wright squirmed at the thought. He picked out his words carefully, like ammunition. "Hi, honey, bought you a present." Then she'd say, "What is it?" thinking maybe he'd picked up a candy bar or a magazine for pennies. And he'd say, "Something to make things a little easier around here in the mornings. . . ." And she'd . . . .

He shuddered. She'd blow her cork is what she'd do. After sitting all morning watching them everlasting give-away programmes on TV, she'd be mad anyway because they couldn't afford fur coats and sets of Worcester china and all that garbage. And then she'd see they were going to have to manage on ten bucks less and she'd slaughter him. The hand holding the pan became suddenly cold and he stuck it in his pocket, hunching his arm awkwardly over the parcel. It must be a couple of weeks since she'd let him . . . now it would be months.

The road climbed gently onto the river bridge. Wright walked faster. There was a place in the middle where you could look over the broken rail and see your own face shining back up at you, a rippling half-moon on the muddy water. As a kid he'd spent hours and hours there. He reached the place and stood for a moment rubbing his fingers over the criss-crossed initials scratched into the ancient paint. His own must be under there somewhere, maybe about three layers of paint down.

He leaned his face over the rail, relishing the cold bite of the metal on his chin. Below him, the clouded water swept by, each speck of colour flowing under his eyes like a pencil stroke. Water under the bridge. That night Alice had let him, the water had looked the same way, he remembered, as though everything else was moving and he was standing still. And everything had changed. Alice had changed, from a scared kid who sat crying on the riverbank afterwards, while he wanted to get the hell home, into someone who lived in a lousy TV world where all the men were handsome and drove sports cars. She'd changed all right, but he hadn't, although he'd always known he'd never be able to pay her back for what she'd given him that summer night.

Slowly, with infinite wisdom and understanding Wright dangled the parcel over the parapet and let it slide out of his fingers. It curved down, smashing the image of his face, sending bright, transmuted particles of water up and outwards in a momentarily infinite pattern. Then the stream brushed the ripples out of sight under the bridge and Wright turned away, rehearsing the only story it was fair to tell her, of losing the money on a slow horse.

The Best-Laid Plan

Peter Brook hung up the phone and stood for a moment looking at the ridges of perspiration his fingers had made on the receiver. His head seemed empty except for the rushing of the blood in his ears. Three weeks overdue and not a sign. Not even a *hint*.

He realised that Old Man Barrett was repeating himself.

"Come on, Brook. Them letters won't sort themselves."

"Sure, Mr. Barrett. Sorry."

He went back to the tall desk which was covered with the midmorning litter of agency mail. He stood there, his eyes and hands going through the automatic motions while inwardly he raced round and round the familiar squirrel cage. Three weeks overdue. It wasn't just a chance any more. It was certain. She was pregnant.

Barrett's voice cawed in on his thoughts again.

97

"Since when was Mr. Stanley on the tenth floor? For Chris-sakes, do the job right, can't you. Why they hire you college kids in the summer is beyond me."

Brook cleared his mind of all thought while the old man's tobacco breath gusted about him and the hairy, liver-spotted hands made their swoops into the mail he had just sorted. The breath and the hands went away and the voice dwindled to a background mutter. Brook set his mind free again and it raced to the next frustration.

Why did it have to be Molly Arnold? A skinny, scared kid who didn't know enough to look after herself. Why hadn't it been Janet or Louise or . . . he hesitated . . . no, it could never have been Grace Meredith. What she'd done for him hadn't been risky at all, had hardly been feminine for that matter. And there weren't any others. The thought stung him. Trapped—by the fourth woman he'd gone with. And you couldn't really count Grace Meredith. It was a lousy track record for a guy of twenty. Why, to hear some of the other fellows talk . . . .

The thought led him into the next blind alley. How could he be sure *he* had knocked her up? He escaped for a moment into a blaze of anger. He wasn't with her every minute. If she was like most women, it could have been anybody, any one of ten guys.

Barrett was saying, "Do you think you can answer the tele-phone while I'm making the rounds? I know it's a lot to ask . . . ."

"Sure, Mr. Barrett." Brook kept his voice polite, proud of his icy control. He wouldn't let the crabby old sonofabitch know he was worried—that would be murder. He toyed with the outgoing mail, biding his time until Barrett had gone, puffing and wheez-ing over his armful of letters. Then he went over to the swivel chair by the phone and sat down. He swung from side to side, keeping his body just out of synchronization with his mind so that the heavy weight of his worry was outside his body, not lying in his chest.

Slowly, his interrupted thought came back to him. How could he *know* he had knocked her up? He tried to recapture his first, fine anger but failed. For crying out loud, she wasn't a pushover, she was a nice kid. A nice kid. He allowed his mouth to form an ironic sneer. A nice kid. Then what was he?

Impulsively he reached for the phone, dialled nine for an outside connection and then Molly's number. A voice said "Good-morning, Commercial Bank."

He asked for Molly's local and after two purrs on the line, her voice said "Savings Department."

"Molly, it's Peter." He couldn't muster enough self-confidence for "Pete" or her favourite, "Petie."

"Peter. What's the matter?"

Her voice had sunk to a nervous whisper.

"Nothing. Nothing new, anyway."

The line fell silent between them and he cursed himself for having called her. What could possibly have changed inside ten minutes.

"I just wanted to say . . ." the treacly words wouldn't come to his lips and he ended lamely ". . . hello."

"What's the good of talking?" she asked. It sounded rehearsed.

"Well, I'd hardly put 'hello' down as talking. It's just one lousy word."

Another long, soughing pause fell between them and then her voice came back again, honest this time, spontaneous.

"Peter, what are we going to *do*?"

Her fear caught him up, like a roller coaster.

"I don't know. I just don't know," he said.

There was silence again and he could imagine how she looked at this moment: lower lip drawn in between her teeth, dark circles under her eyes, her bland prettiness distorted, lost. He spoke slowly, making his voice deeper than it need have been.

" Listen, I'll think of something. I'll see you tonight. O.K?"

"O.K. . . . and Petie . . . ."

"Yeah?"

"I'm sorry . . . ."

"Don't be crazy, Molly. 'Bye."

"Good-bye."

He hung up the phone and moved away from it, impatiently. What in hell could he do? He wasn't a doctor, he didn't know a placenta from a ventricle. If he did. . . . If he'd taken medicine instead of radio and TV arts . . . oh, brother, would it be sweet . . . .

He brought himself back from the luxury of frustration, back to the here and now of guilt. What could he do? They had to bring on her period. Weren't there pills for that? Female pills? Maybe Molly would know. He took a step towards the phone, then realised the idiocy of his idea. If there were pills like that, she'd have taken them already. She wasn't stupid.

An operation. That was the obvious answer, he thought, and the realization filled him with a shuddering fury. Great idea. Just dandy. Who? Where? And what the hell with? This was Canada for Chrissakes, not Sweden, or Japan or some civilized country. You had to hunt around like a thief in the night to find somebody, and then it cost you an arm and a leg. Oh sure it was a great idea, like the mice deciding to bell the cat.

He paced up and down, organizing his thoughts. Assets: two dollars and change to last him till payday. Three hundred and eighty dollars saved against his fall expenses, but he couldn't get his hands on that, his Mother had stuck it in her savings account. Other assets, negligible. A five-stringed banjo, two decent suits and a sportscoat. Oh yes, and a high paying future in the glamorous, goddamn world of Radio TV Arts. Probably starting as assistant producer in some half-assed local station at three thousand a year. Liabilities: One foetus, developing hour by hour inside a face-in-the-crowd girl who worked in a bank. One widowed mother.

He would need money. That was obvious. Whether he was going to do something for the girl or just blow town, he would need money. For a while his mind rested against the comforting blank wall of where he would get the money. But this deceit soon failed him and he came back to his prime worry: what to do?

The answer came to him, complete, swimming into his memory whole—the plot of an English movie he had watched on TV. A hot, very hot bath, and gin. A real old-fashioned remedy. And it worked. It had worked in the movie and it probably worked all the time. Like all those other old wives' tales—the custom of putting white mould on an open cut, dating back from God knows when in Spain. Hadn't penicillin been shown to come from that same mould? And foxgloves for heart problems. Didn't doctors get a heart drug from foxgloves these days?

He'd read about both cases in an article in the *Reader's Digest*. The abortion technique hadn't been in the feature, naturally. But it would work. He was sure of it. Now, all he needed was the money—just a little money.

Barrett came back, walking even slower than usual, mopping his forehead with a paisley handkerchief. Brook bounced up and turned the chair towards him, his face a picture of concern.

"Here, Mr. Barrett, sit down. You look beat."

The old man sat. He was big, Brook noticed, and had been soldierly once upon a time.

"I sure am. Doing the work of two men's enough to get anybody beat."

Brook clucked and mumbled the blend of sympathy and apologies that it took to get the old man calm enough to let him make the next delivery, the twelfth floor where the television department had its languid headquarters. It was the only place in the agency where the people might understand his language, might just extend him the sympathy, the money he needed.

Within minutes he was there. He smiled the regulation smile at the receptionist and she smiled back. And then he was on his own, his mail stacked neatly on his left arm, his right hand holding his next delivery. He by-passed the senior producer's office, nervously dropping his mail on the secretary's desk. He found his breath almost gone, his heart seeming to batter it out of his chest. No use losing his head. It had to be someone closer to his own age. It had to be one of the assistants. Please God, let one be in.

One of them was: Jake Stanley, an extravagantly sloppy young man who worked mostly at recording sessions. He was young and talented and expendable, the ideal man to front for the producer. When Brook came level with his office, Stanley was lying back in his chair, out of sight behind the enormous crepe soles of his shoes. Brook came firmly into the office, determined that he would not look slimy, no matter what happened.

"Good afternoon. There's a letter from New York for you."

"No foolin'." Stanley's voice was bantering, not malicious. Brook moved ahead.

"No fooling. You always seem to get interesting mail."

"Invoices, man. I get invoices from all over," Stanley said. He swung his feet down and picked up his letter, going through the routine of holding it up to the light, tapping one end on the desk and tearing the other end completely off. He waved the yellow page that lay inside.

"See, invoices. Hungry hands outstretched for bread—some days their little voices fairly break your heart."

Brook laughed gratefully, knowing that anyone with a sense of fun was bound to be sympathetic. He began to talk, moving honestly from step to step until his final request. It was no contest. Stanley sent a secretary downstairs to cash a cheque for the necessary twenty. While he was waiting for the girl to come back, he made fun of Brook gently and Brook smiled and shifted from foot to foot and did all the things a radio TV arts third year student could be expected to do. Inside he was calm. He was getting the money. Everything would be all right now.

Stanley said, "Man, I gotta hand it to you, standing by the broad. Most cats cut out."

"I wouldn't want to do that," Brook said. "It's my fault she's in the mess."

"Yeah, sure buddy," Stanley said. "But wait'll after bath night. Nothing. You know what I mean? Like this gin jazz was put out by the distillers. It's nowhere baby."

The girl came back with the money and Stanley handed it over, not counting it.

"Here. Put the lid on the population explosion."

"Thank you . . . . I'll pay you back on payday." Brooks was very near to tears now, suddenly with the money, the answer in his hands.

"Yeah, sure. Like—remember me in your prayers," Stanley said. He looked embarrassed and Brook left him, quickly, nodding gratefully once more.

He was late getting back to the mail room but he took his tongue-lashing passively. It was so very little to pay for the bulk and power of the twenty dollars in his hip pocket. It was going to be all right. All bloody right, all bloody over again.

He called Molly and told her to make an excuse for staying out all night. She wanted to know why but he didn't commit himself. Finally, after a few protests, she admitted that it would be easy to do, she had a great many friends in town. "So pack a suitcase then, and I'll see you at eight."

"Peter"—the voice was pitched low and nervous—"Peter, what are you going to do?"

"Tell you t'night." He clipped it short, businesslike.

"'Bye for now."

"'Bye."

He hung up the phone, feeling strong, decisive. He was again meeting his destiny head on, instead of trying to roll out of its way.

He phoned again, home this time. His mother answered, sounding breathless as she always did, as if surprised that anyone should phone her.

"Hi, Mom, it's Pete. How's it going?"

Everything was fine.

"Yeah, good. Well the reason I called, John Powers, he's one of the guys here, he's having a party up at his cottage tonight. A bunch of fellows are going up there, taking our instruments. I wondered if I could use the car. I'll bring it back tomorrow, after work."

It had all sounded so plausible, he was sure of it. Now he waited while the slow mechanism of refusal whirred into action.

Was it really such a good idea to go partying in the middle of the week? He had a job to consider. He needed his sleep. He shook his head slowly, biting back the frustration and the anger which could have given him away. Her voice went on: had he forgotten that she always shopped on Thursday? she would need the car before he got home tomorrow evening. She would need the car tomorrow morning.

"I could drive home first, then go on to the office."

No, that didn't seem like a very good start to a day's work.

"I'm only working in the mail room, you know. Any grade school kid could do this job with half an eye."

His attitude didn't seem very mature.

If only she knew. Goddamn it. If only she knew. She'd swallow her everlasting dust mop.

"So listen, I have to go now Mom. I'll be home around six and pick up my axe . . . my banjo."

She did a little more chuntering and hung up. Peter waited for the clatter from her end of the line and then laid out all the four letter words he could think of, right into the mouthpiece. This meant no motel. Which in turn meant he'd have to shack up at some hotel someplace. He considered the choices. It couldn't be anywhere fancy. A. Price was against it. B. They wouldn't look very bona fide, turning up on foot. He shelved the decision till later, letting his mind run on to the aftermath of the evening, to freedom, sweet swinging freedom.

The afternoon hung on and on. For a while Brook half expected the phone to ring and Molly to tell him it was all right, it had come. After all, it was going to now, before the day was over. But the phone didn't ring. The only noise in the hot little mail room was old man Barrett's relentless whine. Brook felt sure he would go mad before five o'clock. But at five he suddenly became calm again. He stayed around for ten extra minutes helping Barrett with the ritual cleaning up. The old man said, "You don't have t' stick around. I'll do it."

"No trouble. I'm staying downtown this evening," he said. And his flat inner voice added that he had three hours to kill before the infanticide took place. He noticed with surprise that his hands were trembling.

He left the office building and walked to the greasy spoon where he usually ate lunch on paydays. It was deserted except for the staff, and the waitress looked at him oddly. He ordered a plain cheese sandwich and a milk shake. He could have eaten more but the thought of it made him feel guilty. With what he had planned for the evening he had no right gorging hamburgers.

He walked over to the streetcar stop. The street was quiet now, the rush-hour traffic dissipated, the low angle of the sun making everything golden. Brook checked the time. Only 6:15. He had an hour and three quarters to kill before he saw her. And of course, he had to buy the jug. He took the first streetcar that came by and rode in towards a more central part of town, close to the city's skid row. The liquor store operatives shouldn't ask too many questions here, he thought.

He walked into the store at a few minutes to seven and went boldly to the side counter to write out his order. He had never bought gin before and wondered what kind to get. After some thought, he settled on an expensive English brand. After all, this was an old-country remedy, better use the original stuff. He took his order to the desk and pushed it through the wicket, together with one of his two tens. The cashier looked at him without speaking, until Brook felt his colour beginning to rise. "Something the matter?" he asked, as innocently as he could manage.

"Guess not." The cashier took his money and punched the slip through on the register. He slid the slip and the change back through to Brook.

"Some of you guys of twenty-one look awful goddamn young, 'f you ask me," he said.

Brook huffed out a polite snort of laughter and picked up the slip, trying to keep his hand from shaking. A clerk initialled the order and brought out the bottle, swinging it towards him so that he could check the label. It was a label he had only seen in ads. He nodded silently and the man wrapped it and pushed it over to him.

"Thanks," Brook said. He turned away and walked to the door, feeling self-conscious under the weight of eyes on his back.

Then he set out to walk the fifteen blocks to his rendezvous with Molly. He calculated it would take exactly the right amount of time. He wondered what his mother would think, as he hadn't come home for his banjo. She wouldn't miss that; he'd have to think of some story to tell her tomorrow.

Molly was waiting for him at the corner, her hands clasped in front of her on the handle of her suitcase. To Brook's eyes, the pose shrieked pregnancy and his heart jumped again. What hope was there if she was already *acting* that way? She didn't see him until he was half a block away. She let go of the suitcase with one hand and walked towards him, her whole body listing with the weight. She spoke first, her face drawn down with the words.

"Peter, what's the big secret about?"

He closed the last two paces and took her by the arm.

"We're going to take a hotel room and straighten out this whole business," he said.

"How?" Her question was plaintive but it angered him.

"You'll see," he said, and wondered why her paleness should seem a personal rebuke.

He took the suitcase from her and headed back towards the corner, and the streetcar stop.

105

She leaned around him as they walked, staring at the wrapped bottle under his arm.

"Why did you buy that bottle?"

"I'll explain later," he said. His anger was pounding with every pulse beat. Couldn't she keep quiet? Didn't she realize he was doing his best for her?

She stopped walking, holding absolutely still, like a child playing frozen tag. He walked on for a few steps then paused and looked back at her.

"Come on . . . please . . . ."

She shook her head. Brook glanced around quickly to make sure no passers-by were watching. Then slowly he walked back to her and put down the suitcase so that he could hold her arm. She didn't look up at him but he could see that her eyes were filled with tears.

"Come on now Molly, please, honey."

"I know what you want to do," she said.

"No you don't, honestly." He stroked her arm, softly, pleadingly. "Come on, let's get a place to stay, somewhere we can be on our own. Everything will be all right then."

"No, it won't be all right. Nothing's ever going to be all right. I'm going to have a baby."

Her tears had still not fallen and Brook began to feel a little more sure of himself.

Sure she was scared, she had plenty to be scared about. "Don't be frightened. I'll take care of you," he said.

Now she looked up at him, lips drawn thin against her front teeth.

"Will you, Peter?"

"Sure I will." He gave her arm a couple of quick pats. "Sure I will. But you're going to have to trust me."

She smiled then, blinking her eyes to brush away the unshed tears.

"Yes. I guess I have to," she said. And for a second, Brook was in love with her.

"Come on then." He picked up the suitcase again and started away towards the corner. She walked beside him, her hand squeezed under his elbow.

"Let me carry that . . ." she said, indicating the bottle.

106

"Sure." Brook let her take it and they walked on together, quietly.

In the streetcar he opened her suitcase and put the bottle inside. She didn't say very much and Brook just smiled at her, as if that should explain everything. They transferred on to another car and got off a block from the bus terminal. "We'll go to the Barry Arms," Brook said. "They get all the people from the bus depot, no questions asked."

He led her across the street to the hotel, a smoky brick building with a neon sign that stayed on day and night. He opened the steel-framed door for her and they both walked over to the desk. The clerk was a thin-lipped young man, dark and suspicious looking. Brook said, "Evening. Do you have a double room please?"

"Yes, sir." The dark eyes looked deep into his own.

"Good, how much?" Brook didn't realize that asking the price was the legitimate thing. He was only concerned that the room would be more than fourteen dollars, which was all he had left.

"For one night?" The clerk looked at the girl and back at Brook, insolently.

"Yes," Brook said.

"Eight dollars."

"Sounds fine." Brook reached for his billfold.

"You pay in the morning, sir," the clerk said. "You *do* plan to be here all night, I suppose?"

Brook's anger kept him from flushing. "Of course."

"Just wondering, sir. A great number of our patrons have to leave on night-time buses, you understand."

"I see." Brook hesitated a moment and then asked. "This room, it does have a bath, I hope."

He didn't dare look at Molly, he could feel her eyes flaming into him.

"Of course, sir. A four-piece bath."

"Fine." Brook reached for the proffered card and signed in Mr. and Mrs. Broom, Sudbury.

The clerk took the card and read the name, flashing a quick look at Brook's face, as if expecting to find a comparative signature there. Then he took a key from the pigeonholes behind him and pinged the desk bell. A bellhop came forward and led them

107

towards the elevator. Brook tried to put his hand under Molly's elbow but she shrugged him off with a short, hidden motion.

They rode up in silence and the bellhop showed them to the room. He put on the lights and left them, nodding curtly over the quarter Brook handed him. With the door shut, Brook turned to look at Molly. She had sat down on the end of one of the beds and was scuffing her foot back and forth over the pattern in the carpet.

Brook went over and knelt down beside her. She let him put his arms around her waist but went on pushing at the carpet with her foot. He knelt there for perhaps a minute, trying to think of something to say. Finally, he tried "Everything's going to be O.K. Molly, honestly."

"Everything *is* O.K. for you," she said.

"Don't be like that. It's going to be fine. You'll have a nice hot bath and a drink of gin and everything will be fine."

"Oh sure." She sat up very straight now, pushing him off. "And I guess you believe in Santa Claus, too."

He stood up, indignant, tall. "Look, I'm trying to help. There isn't a law in the land that says I have to. I just want to, that's all."

"Thank you very much," she said. Brook hoped she would continue but she said nothing more, just sat, not looking at him. Finally he said, "I'm not in the habit of taking girls to hotel rooms, you know."

"Of course you're not!" she blazed. "It's cheaper to do it in the car."

"God, you're sweet. You know that?"

"I'm pregnant is what I am," she said. She had lost her anger now and was sitting hunched at the end of the bed. Brook went back to her and knelt beside her, his hand on her back, his mouth close to her face. "You don't have to be," he said.

"That's easy to say. It's not so easy to change anything." She pushed a strand of hair away from her face and the action made her look like a schoolgirl. For the second time Brook was moved to tenderness.

"You don't know. Not for sure. You can't know, until you've tried it," he said.

"But it's not right," she said, very quietly.

"It depends how you look at it." Brook was ready for this one, had practised the arguments. "All you're doing is bringing on your period. There's nothing bad about that, is there?"

"Isn't there?" she turned her deep, pale face towards him.

"You know there isn't. Haven't you ever taken anything before when it's been late?"

"It's never been late before . . . it's never had any cause to be late."

All right, Brook thought. She didn't have to twist the knife. He fumbled a second for the flaw in her statement. "Then you don't know whether this is going to work or not," he said, trying to be cheerful.

She shrugged her shoulders. Brook stood up again, making his movements big, decisive. "So let's give it a try then—O.K!" He went to the case and flipped it open to take out the bottle. "Now, why don't you get into a housecoat or something comfortable, and I'll run the tub."

He took the bottle and went into the bathroom. There were two glasses on the ledge, in front of the mirror, and he poured gin into one of them. Then he set the bottle down on the ledge and stood looking at himself in the glass. He was good-looking, he decided. Too dark under the eyes, and his hair too long, he must do something about that, but certainly he was a good-looking, clean-cut kid. The kind of guy a girl shouldn't mind being in a hotel room with. He shook his head pensively at his reflection and stooped to run the tub. It came hot at once, clouds of steam rising from the first gush. Good, he thought. That should work wonders.

He walked back to where she was sitting as he had left her. He handed her the glass and she took it automatically. Slowly she looked up at him.

"Are you going to drink some?"

"No, it's for you," he said.

"I'm scared."

"Don't be. It's just a drop of gin." He patted her hand and she caught his fingers.

"I don't want to drink."

109

"But it's good gin," he said.

"I've never drunk gin before. I've only ever had wine, and that rye you bought me after the show once."

"This is nicer than rye. Smell it." He held the glass to her and she sniffed it obediently.

She wrinkled her nose in disgust. "It smells strong."

"It's nice," he repeated. He lifted the glass to her and sipped. The liquor filled his mouth and throat like a cold flame. He coughed.

"It is strong," she said.

He coughed again, his eyes running. "Not really. It's just that I generally drink rye." He felt ridiculous but reassured. If gin did that to *him* what wouldn't it do to *her*? "Here, try it." He thrust it towards her but she pushed the glass aside.

"Not like that. It needs pop in it. Tonic water or lemon or something. . . ."

She waved her left hand in a vague circle and Brook marvelled at her. She had forgotten her trouble it seemed. Her only concern was her ignorance of gin.

The sound of the water rushing into the tub made him turn suddenly. "Hey, the tub." He dived for the bathroom, deliberately making himself look clumsy. It would help calm her down, he thought. He waved away the steam with his arms high and turned off the tap. The water looked cruelly hot. He felt anxious for the girl's safety. She shouldn't get into that. It was too hot, he couldn't ask that of anybody. He tried to sneak a look at himself in the mirror, in his new compassionate mood, but the glass was misted over and he saw only a blurry movement.

He went back into the room, his shoulders hunched a little in defeat. Molly was still sitting on the foot of the bed, but she was looking at him with genuine interest in her face. Like she was watching television, he thought. He smiled at her, a wry twist of his mouth, and walked by her to the window. Below him were the backyards of Chinatown, brick-walled yards filled with lines of grey washing, leggy sumac trees and rubbish. In one of them children sat in the shadow, dispiritedly. The sight of them reminded him of his purpose. He turned to her, smiling a little more honestly now.

110

"Listen, we can't drink that stuff on its own. I'll go down and get something to mix it with."

"Don't let anybody see you," she said.

"I don't think I'll meet anyone I know, not in this joint," he said, and then realizing his error he backtracked. "Not unless they're here incognito the same as us."

She was sitting still again, watching him. He went up and patted her on the shoulder.

"Listen, why'nt you get into something comfortable while I'm gone. Then we'll be ready . . . for the tub, I mean."

She said nothing, but he held her gaze until finally she said, "All right." Then he left her.

He went to the hotel cigar stand but they had no soft drinks so he went out to the street and down to the drug store. The sun was very low now, giving the street an alien look, making it part of a new city he had never seen before. He felt cosmopolitan and raffish buying a carton of pop and exchanging a few words with the withered old Chinaman behind the counter. When he re-turned, he didn't mind the frankly hostile looks the elevator operator gave him. He was his own man tonight, for the first time in his life and he was enjoying it.

He tapped at the door of the room and after a brief pause Molly opened it, showing only her face. He closed the door and looked at her, his eyes overflowing with his new authority. She met his gaze for a moment then looked down modestly. She was wearing a cheap cotton housecoat, newish still and colourful. He could tell she felt pretty in it.

"That's pretty," he said. And she said, "Thank you."

He stood, awkwardly for a while, then put the pop down on the chest of drawers.

"I didn't know what would be best. I bought some of every-thing."

"They say lime's nice," she said.

"Lemon-lime do?" he pulled out the green bottle.

"O.K." She pressed her hands together, breathlessly. He was reminded of a child waiting for a scolding. God, she was a touch-ing little thing when you thought about it. He opened the bottle and added pop to the first glass of gin. Then he got another glass

111

from the bathroom and poured himself the same size drink. He noticed that most of the steam had gone from the bathroom. It would soon be time to start.

He gave her the drink and they sipped, not looking at one another. The pop masked most of the gin flavour.

"Hey, this is nice," he said. He was standing, but gradually the tension passed out of him until he found himself sitting on the bed beside her.

"Drink up!" he urged.

"Mom would kill me." It burst out of her, complete.

Brook smiled consolingly.

"Mine'd just die. Honest to God. Right there on the spot. Boom."

She giggled, a quick single note. Then she covered her mouth and looked serious again.

"No, I mean it. She always drummed it into us girls. Don't. Don't. That's all there is to it. Don't."

She fixed her eyes on him, suddenly embarrassed. He rose to the occasion.

"It must be hard for them. I mean, they want us all to do well. They don't want any foul-ups. You can understand them."

"Oh, Petie." She pushed against him, as if she were trying to bury herself in his chest. "What are we going to do if this doesn't work? What'll we do?"

"It's going to work." Brook emptied his glass in three swallows, feeling the taste grow more bitter with every mouthful. "Drink up and we'll have another, then we'll try that tub."

"Peter, I'm scared." She thrust herself harder against him, her body tense.

"Don't be." He set his glass down and put his arms around her shoulders. No use forcing her to drink faster, it might just make her sick. That would be no good. He patted her shoulder and her body began to soften.

"That's better. There's a good girl."

"Peter . . . ." Her face was raised towards his, eyes full of stupid, unreasoning devotion. "Peter . . . you're wonderful to me."

"Don't be silly," he said gruffly.

"No, Petie. Really, I mean it. Otherwise I wouldn't have . . .

112

have let you . . . ."

He drew a deep, gratified breath. "Molly. You know how I feel about you, don't you?"

She nodded, her head bumping happily against his chest. He was reminded of puppy dogs wagging their tails. Gently he tried to lead back to the reason they were together.

"Drink up and we'll have another."

"Both of us? You won't make me drink it on my own?"

"Promise."

"All right then." She lifted the glass in both hands, like a baby and drank thirstily. He took the glasses and poured them two more drinks the same size, opening another bottle of pop indifferently. He gave it to her and she took it without looking, her eyes fixed on his.

"Cheers," he said.

She nodded and half smiled. She didn't drink. Her hand reached out for his hand, pulled him down beside her. He sat close to her, and they kissed, a hungry crushing together of aching mouths. Brook felt the old excitement race through him. He slipped his free hand under her housecoat. Her breast was warm and hard to his touch, the nipple high. It wouldn't matter. It couldn't make a bit of difference now—his mind shouted aloud to him—this is your chance for a bit of real fancy loving.

Then she tore herself away, rolling away from him and standing the other side of the bed.

"Peter!" She was flushed, more beautiful than he could ever remember her.

"Peter, how could you?"

"Because I love you," he said slowly.

She untensed, muscle by muscle and her face shone with wonder. Inch by inch she flowed back towards him. He reached and took her glass away from her, put both glasses on the floor out of the way. And still she came towards him.

"Petie. You've never said that to me before."

"I've never said it to anyone before."

"Peter. Mean it. Please mean it. I love you so much Peter."

"I mean it. I love you."

It was true. How else could a man feel? he asked himself. She

113

was a sweet, clear-eyed, honest kid and she'd let him and now she was in trouble. But she wasn't blaming him. He drew her face to his and kissed her again, slowly and deep, tongue upon tongue.

"Darling, I'm scared . . . ." She whispered it to him as he lay beside her, his hand flat on the concavity of her belly.

"Don't be. I'll be gentle."

"I know you will. I love you." She made a quick kiss at his cheek. "I mean about the bath. I'm scared. It isn't right."

"I know. I don't think it is either. Not really." He took his hands from her and sat up on the bed hunching his knees in front of him, his arms clasped around them.

"But what will we do?" She lay there very still, her eyes enormous in the dusk.

Brook looked at her for a long time, the words building themselves up painfully one after another into his pronouncement.

"I'll tell you what we'll do. We'll *have* the little guy. We'll get married. O.K? Tomorrow morning we'll go home and tell our folks. They'll weep and wail but we'll get married."

His voice left him. The rest of the words died in his throat. They would get married and live happily ever after, the three of them. He meant it, but there was no way he could get the words out. Instead, he took her hands and drew her towards him. Her eyes were shining with happy tears.

"Darling Petie. Darling."

"Baby. Baby. Baby." Brook said and the sound of his voice reminded him of Jake Stanley. And as Molly lowered herself flat onto the bed, his mind was racing around fresh squirrel cages. Could his mother stop him getting married? Could he get a better job at the agency? Could he expect Stanley to make a wedding present of the twenty dollars? Slowly the presence of his desire forced his brain clear of thoughts and he drew her to him in the triumphant act of love. And in the bathroom the tub of water began its slow temperature decline from scalding heat to body heat, in rather the same fashion as a happy marriage.

114

The
Cucumber
Contract

It was fun all that July.

Fun, every evening in that perfect hour when the sun hung
from the branches of the maples along the edge of the cucumber
field and the sky was laced with fine strands of cirrus.

Fun, bending and stretching over the cucumber vines with
their papery orange flowers and warty, green fingers of fruit.

Every evening as Bailey knelt and worked in the sandy earth
he blessed the good fortune that had come to them now, in the
discipline of their first summer in the country.

After supper, Anne would start out again beside him, although her faster picking soon moved her ahead of him to where
she had to call out the questions, the regular questions. She
would nod and listen to his answers and pick with a gypsy's
practised ease, rifling the vines of the tiniest of the fruit, infant

cucumbers that would end up as baby dill pickles in some Montreal gourmet shop.

Bailey would answer her questions, talking sturdily about the day's confrontations, the meetings and the politics which always seemed to work out to his advantage, out here under his own acre and a half of sky. The hour would pass. It ended perhaps a minute earlier each day as the year grew older. The sun would slip from sight and the first mosquitoes of the evening would find them.

"Here come the skitters," Bailey said, as he always did.

"They never bother me," Anne said, still picking.

Bailey's mouth opened to shape "You're lucky." Then he stopped with the words unspoken, remembering the talk Dr. Andrews had given him about Anne's chemical balance, the subtle differences in chemistry that gave rise to her condition. Bailey knew he would rather suffer the mosquito bites than share Anne's chemistry.

"I'm going to quit right here," he said. "Mark the place for me while I empty this bucket."

He waited while Anne straightened up, tall and golden with the tan she had acquired these last six weeks, working daily in the field. Very slowly, she walked back to him.

She stood looking absently about her for the yellow over-sized cucumbers that meant one of them had missed a vine or two on the last pass up the field. Bailey wished she would look at him, perhaps reach out and touch him as she stood so close in her sleeveless cotton blouse and the striped shorts he had bought for her when she was in the hospital. But she did not.

She said, "You take the sacks up to the barn, I'll pick a minute longer."

He went to the first sack and shook the contents down until there were eight or so inches of slack at the top for him to grip. A bunt with the knee, a turn of the body and the sack was up on his shoulder, moulding itself to the contour of his back and neck while he paced methodically over the crumbly soil towards the barn. This was the hardest part of the work, the part he most enjoyed. Carrying out this labour gave him pride in his height and strength. Six foot one and a flat-bellied one hundred and eighty pounds. That was a man's build and it was

118

good to be doing a man's work, instead of playing office. Out here, on his own land, using his muscles, he could be proud of himself and free.

Almost free. As he walked back for another sack he could see Anne crouching beside another vine, picking mechanically. From a distance, with the sky's last colour soaking into her blue blouse, she seemed like some flower, on the point of standing and opening for the world to admire. Her sickness no more than a shadow, behind her, out of sight.

Bailey carried all the sacks down to the barn and stacked them inside, by the door, checking that each of them was marked with his name and address, and the pickle contract number, lettered in Anne's large scrawly script with a felt pen he had begged from an art director at the office.

Then he walked back up the edge of the field. Anne was still picking, wanting to finish her row ready for a fresh start in the coolness of early morning.

Bailey crouched and picked towards her down the row. It was just a token move. Anne quickly finished the row while he picked intermittently between swipes at the mosquitoes with their dedicated, dental-drill hum.

"There," she said, swinging her bucket towards him. "That's enough for today."

"Well I guess so." Bailey took the bucket and dropped his own few in on top of them. "You know you've picked eight sacks since the truck came."

"And they were small ones, almost all of them." She walked slowly, pressing her right hand into her back, just above the pelvis. He held out his free hand to her and she took it, linking fingers with him in an immediate little-girlish gesture that made him smile, even though she had forgotten to take off her work gloves and the sandy cloth was harsh to his touch.

"The little ones are the best," he said. "Pick a ton of them and we get two hundred and thirty beautiful dollars."

She laughed and swung her arm in a little jerking gesture that made his fingers jolt. "Have you ever seriously considered just how many of those tiny little cucumbers it would take to make up a ton?"

"Mountains of them," he said happily.

"I know."

"So if you think you're going to get off lightly, you're not."

"As I remember, eight years ago, I promised to love, honour and obey. There was nothing in the contract about picking cukes from dawn to dusk."

Her voice was happy, tired but with a playful lilt to it. He stopped and turned to hold her to him and kiss her.

Without awkwardness she turned her face at the last moment so that his kiss landed on her cheek, as if she were royalty receiving homage. "Sex among the cucumbers. What will the neighbours say, Mr. Bailey?"

They laughed and walked the rest of the way in silence, Anne tugging her hand free once more to reach down and pluck an oversize cuke they had missed the day before.

"Those big ones steal all the goodness from the little ones," she said.

"It's the same the whole world over." Bailey clowned, loving her, loving the night that was forming about them, loving his life.

They stood for a minute or two, checking over the bags, estimating how many pounds they had picked in the forty-eight hours since the last collection. Then Bailey switched off the light in its white enamel, coolie hat shade and they shut the half-door of the barn and walked to the house.

The heat had gathered inside, stacked against the screen door so it seemed to pour out over the sill to meet them.

Anne said, "Lets sit on the porch, I'll just tub and change."

"O.K.," Bailey said, as he did every night. "That's a good idea. I'll make some iced tea."

Anne went on up the stairs and Bailey washed his hands at the kitchen sink and got out the pitcher for iced tea.

As he made the tea he drew himself a cold glass of water and gulped it down, wishing there was a cold beer in the house or better still a crisp gin and tonic with its arctic blueness in the glass and its absolutely symmetrical matching to the peaks and valleys of his very special thirst. But there was not. So he made the tea, making it strong so it would keep its flavour under the burden of ice he would add when it was a little cooler. He set out the glasses on a tray, frosting them with ice first, then decorating them with bright wheels of lemon.

By the time it was ready Anne was out of the tub, dressed in a light cotton nightgown and smelling of dusting powder. She came over and looked at his arrangements with the tea. "I wonder what it would be like with cucumber slices," she mused.

Bailey laughed. "Terrible, if you ask me. But since we've got a whole acre of them, I'm ready to try."

"I'll do it." She brushed by him towards the refrigerator, unconscious of the pleasure her nearness gave him. "You go and have your tub and I'll slice the vittles."

"O.K.," he said. "I'll be right down."

By the time he had cleaned up she was sitting on his chaise-longue in the screened-in porch with the little amber candle burning in its glass container. The tea things were beside her, the jug heavily misted with moisture. Beyond the screens the mosquitoes were buzzing and somewhere a whippoorwill was complaining. The scent of stocks and the minty freshness of bergamot lay on the air.

Bailey was pleasantly cool after his tub but the heat of the day was still within reach, waiting to pounce if he were fool enough to exert himself any more. Anne was relaxed but somehow strangely formal in her high-necked nightgown. "You may pour, Benjamin," she said gravely.

Bailey carried on the play. "Yes m'lady." He filled the glasses with ice cubes and poured the already sweetened tea, squeezing more lemon into each glass. He passed Anne's to her, making it a gesture that deserved a flourish of trumpets.

Then he sat with his own glass, raised it to her formally and sipped.

Outside, above the lawn, fireflies flashed their primeval neon.

A car passed up the road, moving slowly, as tired in the heat as the horse it had replaced.

Anne was the first to speak. "Why didn't we come to this sooner, Ben? I've wondered and wondered this last month or two." Her voice had a contentment in it that made Bailey blink quickly and catch his breath before he could speak. He thought —*Because your mother took her own sweet time about dying and we didn't have the down payment*. But he said, "We couldn't afford it, dear. That's the trouble with things I guess, you have to wait for them and sometimes the waiting is too long."

121

"It almost was," Anne said. "Another year in town and it might have been. But out here it's easier. The whole place is relaxing, and those cucumbers . . . . Imagine—our first summer and we're holding a multi-dollar cucumber contract."

"Never underestimate the power of advertising," Bailey said. "If you hadn't seen the ad and phoned we wouldn't have known how easy it is."

Anne stretched out her hands, twisting her arms and forcing her shoulders forward, like a lean cat stretching in the sun.

"Wasn't I clever Ben, the whole thing is so gloriously mindless."

"You're right," Bailey said. "That's what I like about it, too."

He waited in silence then, knowing Anne would carry the conversation tonight. She felt good and it made him almost too happy.

"I've always felt bad about not having children." Her voice was musing now; it would change, Bailey knew that. She would follow the thread of her own argument at its own tempo. With more excitement she went on. "I knew how much you wanted children. You'd have been a wonderful father."

It was on the tip of Bailey's tongue to say "We could adopt some, you know." But he kept his peace. This was Anne's monologue. His part in it was to listen.

"Anyway, today, out there on the patch I was thinking. You know what those cukes are?"

He said nothing and she repeated her question, wanting him to join in now.

"Tell me," he said.

"They're our children. Instead of two or three kids we've got hundreds of thousands of knobbly, green little children that will go forth to the world in twelve-ounce jars and spread joy and delight for years to come. Especially with ham or cheese, of course."

"Of course," Bailey said. His hand was cold from holding the glass so he set it down and wiped his palm on his pant leg. Then he got to his feet impulsively and went to the side of her chair. This time she did not turn her mouth away from him.

When he woke next morning she was not beside him. Her

pillow was dented and there was a memory of her talcum in the bed. He sat up and reached for the clock. It showed 7:10 but the alarm had gone off at 4:30.

He called once, as he always did. "Anne, are you there?" There was no answer. He got out of bed and walked to the window. Yes, she was out there, her hair tied behind her with a brave little ribbon, crouched halfway down a row, a full sack of cucumbers standing close to her.

Bailey smiled and went to prepare for his day.

When he came downstairs he found his breakfast ready. The table was laid and cereal and china set out. The milk and half a grapefruit, sugared just the way he liked it, were in the refrigerator. He plugged in the kettle for instant coffee and sat down to eat.

By eight o'clock he was ready to leave. He walked down the edge of the field to where Anne was working.

She stood up and came towards him, arching her back. "Lazy-bones," she said. "Look, I've picked one sack already *and* started another."

"I'm out of my class," he said. He stooped and plucked himself a cucumber, wiping the sand from it with his hand, then biting into it, savouring the hidden coolness that lay deep within the sun-warmed outer layer. "You do put up a very nice cucumber, Mrs. Bailey."

"Well, I haven't had any complaints," she said.

In the morning light she did not look as calm and well as she had the evening before. There was a hint of the old puffiness and the sunlight was making tiny crinkles at the corners of her eyes. She looked every year of her thirty-seven.

Bailey switched his mind back to something casual, anything. "Say, aren't the pickle people supposed to give us part of our cheque sometime soon?"

"They said so." Anne frowned. "They said they paid the first part when the crop was about half-done. Then we get the big cheque later when it's all finished."

"I think it's high time you got some recognition anyway," Bailey said. "If they don't come across with some money by Saturday I'm going to get some out of the bank and buy us both a big dinner downtown."

"What a lovely idea," Anne said. "We can go to the Bull and Bush, they have an English cook who does wonderful things with cucumbers."

Bailey laughed and said that he thought he had seen his share of cucumbers. Then he gave her a quick light kiss on the cheek and was gone, back through the dust to his car and down the concession road to the highway and his office.

He was in a meeting when she phoned. Fortunately in his own office so that she reached him. "Darling, you'll never guess what. . . ."

"What?" His lightness came out very much like petulance. Green and Lonsdale were sitting staring at him, silently waiting for him to complete his call. "The cheque came! When the men came to pick up the cukes, they gave me a cheque and you'll never guess how much it's for."

"I've no idea, is it much?" He made a disarming little gesture with his free hand. Green smiled, Lonsdale only looked at his wristwatch.

"It's for eighty dollars. Eighty whole dollars. Isn't that great!"

"That's fantastic, congratulations. I guess we can move up our plans from Saturday to tonight."

"Not tonight. I'll do something special here."

Lonsdale was scribbling a note on his pad and showing it to Green. Bailey felt the old familiar jolting start in his throat. He said, "That'll be swell dear. Listen, can I call you back, I've got some people with me."

"Ask them if they'd like a bushel of lovely cukes," she said and hung up in the middle of her laugh.

Bailey set the phone down firmly and sat up straight. "Sorry for the interruption, our little business has just declared its first dividend."

Green smiled. Lonsdale said "That's nice" and went on with the words he had been uttering when the phone rang.

The two men were in his office until almost one o'clock. Bailey was on pins and needles to phone Anne and make sure she knew how pleased he was, but when he finally had his office to himself there was no answer at home. He let the phone ring ten times, in case she was somewhere close to the house, within earshot. There was no answer even then.

Reluctantly he hung up and went out into the bleaching heat to cross the street for lunch.

He ate his usual sandwich and drank his buttermilk, wondering all the time whether Anne was outside in the heat, picking. Surely not. Surely she would rest from eleven till three as she always did, stretched out on the porch with a library book and the inevitable pitcher of tea.

He phoned again as soon as he got back to his office. There was still no reply. With mounting concern he left the phone and returned to his business day, half his mind wondering whether to call up the neighbour, Mrs. Rudd, and ask her to look in on Anne. Once he even picked up the phone to call but changed his mind after dialling the first three numbers and dialled his home instead.

At four thirty there was still no reply and he could stand the suspense no longer. He told his secretary he was out making a store check of the shelf-facings enjoyed by his client's soap powder. She smiled at him without voicing her disbelief and said she would see him in the morning.

He ran the last few steps to his car, slipping out of his jacket and throwing it over the back seat as he started the motor. He was home within forty minutes. Anne's car was parked in front of the house. She was not in the cucumber field and as far as Bailey could judge from the driveway she had picked only one more bag of cucumbers. Her day had obviously been spent elsewhere.

His breath was hurting his chest as he opened the door and let himself in. He could not even call out, the pulse in his throat would have smashed the words.

He went through to the living-room, and found her.

She was unconscious, breathing raggedly.

Beside her on the coffee table stood a full bottle of tonic water. The gin bottle was on the floor beside her. It was empty.

Bailey stooped and patted her face until she stirred and opened her eyes, peering out at him as if from prison. Then she swore, once, flat and short, and closed her eyes again. Bailey stood up straight, looking down at her from all the height he could command, willing himself far away from the perfumed mouth with the smeared lipstick.

Then he stooped to take off her shoes and place her more comfortably on the chesterfield. She swore again, in her sleep this time and he turned away from her, to the phone.

Doctor Andrews' answering service took the call. They would contact him; if it were really that urgent he would come over. He had given them Bailey's name as a man who might need emergency help.

Bailey thanked the girl and hung up the phone. Then he walked around the kitchen, re-creating the sequence of events from the scraps of evidence that lay about him.

First clue was the pickle company's envelope. It had been ripped open in excitement, judging by the way it was torn.

Then there was the champagne. He found it in the refrigerator. Domestic pink champagne, the stuff of camp musical comedy.

Bailey took it out and weighed it in his hand, wanting to hurl it the length of the room and shatter it against the wall with its prim little collection of horse brasses that reminded him how other people ordered the impedimenta of their own lives.

That was what she had done, of course. Bought champagne. Full, herself, of the same bubbling exuberance she would find under this cork she had walked into the liquor store to buy champagne.

He could imagine her pleasure as she stepped into the air-conditioned coolness and found herself before the echoing rows of displayed bottles. She would make her choice as much by feel as by appearance. She would pick up the bottles, one at a time, weighing, comparing, enjoying the inference of magic that surrounded the bottles themselves.

And then when her mind was made up it had been so simple an addition to ask for gin as well.

He put the champagne back in the refrigerator and walked back to her. Yes, she had enjoyed her shopping. Had savoured even the delicious procrastination of stopping at the drug store and buying tonic water. She would have known when she bought it that she would never use it to adulterate the pleasure of the gin.

He looked at her again, checking that she was not in danger of regurgitating. A lot of them . . . he made himself stop and take the sentence at its full value. A lot of alcoholics died that way. But she seemed all right. Her face was flushed and her hair was damp with perspiration, strands of it pasted over her brow like pencil marks or odd tribal scars.

Bailey went upstairs to wash.

Doctor Andrews arrived soon after, without having bothered to phone first.

"I guessed what had happened," he said easily. "How long's it been? Let me see, April wasn't it, the last time?"

"April, yes," Bailey said.

"Four months. That's not as long, is it."

Bailey agreed that it was not as long.

The doctor prepared the syringe, the big one, with vitamins and stimulants. The one they called "The Cocktail," the one that cost twenty-five dollars.

"She's looking well. Been working outside I guess," Andrews said. He was still young enough to be hearty.

"We're growing cucumbers. We have a contract with the pickle company," Bailey explained.

The doctor said "I see," in a tone which said that he did not see.

He made a note to himself in his looseleaf book then put the book back into his pocket and closed up his bag, pitching the used syringes into the bottom of it. After a while he left.

Bailey sat on the edge of the chesterfield and waited until the car had paused and turned at the bottom of the driveway and gone into the descending harmonics of leaving. Then he picked up Anne in his arms. She was limp, a dead weight. Carefully, pressing each tread of the stairs very carefully, he carried her up and set her down on the bed. It was warm in the bedroom and he very carefully undressed her. She had become a little more aware of what was going on but did nothing to help or hinder him, just lolling in his arms like a rag doll.

She lay as he had placed her and he covered her with a single sheet. Then he smoothed away the damp hair from her face and went downstairs, As he always did he searched her purse. It contained fifty-eight dollars. He calculated that she must have bought at least two other bottles of gin. Dully he went upstairs again and searched her room. He found the first twenty-sixer in her vanity table. Fighting down the temptation to put it to his own lips he took the bottle to the bathroom and tipped it away, sniffing the fumes deep into his chest in a series of bitter, righteous sighs. Then he rinsed the bottle so there could be no last, single, sticky drop to tempt Anne tomorrow when her hangover hit. He dropped the bottle in the waste container and went back to search for the other bottle. He found it at last. She had tucked it inside the cover of her sewing machine. He drained that one also, feeding his masochism with a calculation of how many rows of cucumbers the spirit represented. How many bendings and stretchings did it take to earn the fifteen dollars Anne had spent?

Finally, he took the bottle of champagne and put it in his car. He would keep it in his office until his secretary had a birthday or until Christmas. Gin was wickedness, you couldn't offer gin to a girl. But champagne was flattering. He would salvage that much from the fiasco.

He slammed the car door and started to walk, aimlessly at first, then out of habit down the well-tramped path to the cucumber field.

Anne's two sacks stood at one side of the field, his bucket at the other, midway down the row where he had left it. Slowly, with control so fierce it made his arms tremble, Bailey forced himself to kneel and begin turning over the cucumber vines in the automatic ritual of the picking.

He found three inch-long cucumbers on the first vine and plucked them with delicate care before his control snapped and he tore the plant out of the ground and beat the heedless earth with it, lashing it around him until the vines tore apart and there was nothing but an inch or two of stem left in his hand. Then he cursed again and wept, suddenly, the tears gouting from his eyes, rolling down his cheeks and splashing into the thirsty earth.

He cried for perhaps a minute, kneading his knuckles into the soil as he sobbed.

Then he brought himself under control again. His tears stopped and his hands unclenched. He sat still for a minute or two, then he moved on to the next cucumber vine and went on with filling his bucket.

A contract was, after all, a contract.

Here's Looking at You

I am a trout.

Don't snigger. It's a living and besides, nothing I've ever heard makes me think that *homo sapiens* is any closer to nirvana than *salmo gairdnerii*.

That statement brought you up short, didn't it. You don't expect a trout to know the jargon of either biology or Buddhism.

Well you don't know me, Mac. I'm not your ordinary rainbow trout, dodging otters and kingfishers and men with hooks covered with horsehair and pheasant fluff. Not me. I work at a Montreal restaurant, one that you probably couldn't afford to eat in, unless you're on an expense account.

Yes, I work here. It may look like a dead-end job to you but I have security. Forty-three of us scull around in this five by three tank with its everlasting air hose burbling away in the corner.

Once in a while some patron comes over and fingers one of

us and the waiter gets the net and hoists us out. I must admit, it's scary. Even now, I worry when my turn comes and I'm carried past those tables full of smirking gluttons. You have that terrible fish-out-of-water feeling, so helpless, sagging there in the net with the noise positively crashing in on your drying nerve ends.

But once you reach the kitchen, you're home free. They tip you back into the holding tank, whisk a Japanese rainbow of comparable size out of the freezer and serve it up to the fool who picked you out. As far as I can tell, the management makes an extra dollar a plate by serving frozen trout, and we, their window dressing, never need replacing.

Of course, you do have the occasional, genuine gourmet who knows he's been fed frozen food. One in particular raised hell. He was a Catholic Father and it was Lent at the time, so I guess he knew the gastronomical score pretty well, but after the maître d' gave him the old "don't-taste-the-same-when-they're-kept-in-chlorinated-city-water" speech, he went away.

And again, once in a while one of the guys in the tank panics when his time comes. The odd one flops right out of the net. And that's curtains. Even the muttonheads who run this place know that a trout is going to get fungus if he flops around on the parquet, so it's out with his entrails and into the pan. I have to admit though, the patrons don't usually look any more ecstatic over a fresh tankmate of mine than they do over the frozen trout.

But I profit from all this. I've learned that the secret of survival is the same as the secret of golf. Relax. Oh, I know, I used to be like all the others. I did all the usual things, the swerving and diving and the final stupid attempt to hide, over behind the air pipe. But it's no use, they come after you with an absolutely pathological firmness once you've been singled out.

Now I play it a little smarter.

Yes, sir!

I've made the trip to the kitchen four times, and frankly, I worry about fungus. Those clods out there don't know a thing about fish. Oh sure, they can whip up an *almondine* as quick as you could blow your nose. But what peasants! In their off hours some of them actually fish for pickerel.

No, it's close to a year since my last trip to the spare tank. And

I don't intend to go out there again. I plan to end my time by dying a natural death, some night when the place is closed. And I think I can make it. I've been figuring the angles. Not like these other dummies in here. They're content to snap up the scraps management throws us every night and spend the rest of their day going around in circles getting stared at.

I reversed the field. I do the staring. I started listening in on conversations too. It's surprising the vibrations you pick up when you press your nose against a sheet of quarter-inch glass. I began hearing answers to questions I'd been asking myself since I was a fingerling. Oh, not the eternal ones—what is life and is there a hereafter and that kind of esoteric jazz. No, I mean the real river-bottom stuff of how to judge your enemy.

My enemy is man, that's obvious. His alimentary tract is the ultimate threat to my existence. But you'd be surprised, not many men are a real threat.

For instance, if you see a guy with a moustache, and pants just a little long and he pauses in front of the tank, you know you're safe. He's a fisherman. If he's alone he will compare you wistfully with the one who broke his line at Camp Lunkerinthelake last summer. If he's in company he'll make whipping motions with his rod arm and he and his companion will laugh a lot. But he's too much of a purist to have you netted for his table.

If you see a woman on her own, you're safe. They're squeamish except for some of the old ones. But by and large, the guy you have to watch for is the balding, little man, with a bigger man in tow.

This place of ours, I guess I should have mentioned, is in the basement of one of Montreal's swankier complexes. We have a raft of agents and publishing and advertising people. Take it from me, some of those guys would eat their own children to impress their clients. Cannibals, that's what they are. When you see one of those operators heading for the tank, that's the time to dive deep and lie at the back, preferably with your head behind the aeration pipe. Once you've learned the trick of the multiple reflections you can still watch from there, in case they do decide on you and drastic action becomes necessary. Usually, though, they go for one of the livelier inmates and it's off to the kitchen for him. Mind you, it's smart to lie low until both men go back to their seats. Many a frisky young tankster has been picked up "for my friend here," just when the net seemed safely out of sight.

Once they've gone, you're safe to go back to the window for more eavesdropping, more information. A lot of the talk is literary, not so much the Who wrote it? kind as the Who's bringing it out? But you do overhear the occasional lecture by one of the anglers—something that tends to glaze the eyes of his companion but which I, of course, prefer to the usual chatter. Once in a while, one of them gets all sympathetic towards us—not knowing about the tank in the kitchen—and one of them once put forward a theory how we might be able to escape. It's long odds, mind you, but I daydreamed about it through one whole, slack Sunday. I'd need to be ordered by a poet who relented once I was in the net, ordered a plastic bag full of water and took me home to live with him in his unused bathtub. Think of that—it's the only possible way out for me.

But I'm a pragmatist. For one thing, there's not a poet in Montreal who could afford to eat in here. And if they did show up, on their agent's expense account for instance, they'd spend the lunch hour smoking moody cigarettes and drinking Dubonnet-on-the-rocks.

True, there are a couple of big league guys in town, Leonard Cohen and Irving Layton. They're big enough to spring me from this tank but they're both publicity conscious enough to bring the Press to take pictures while they fling me dramatically into the St. Lawrence. And believe me, a couple of gillfuls of *that* pollution is enough to poison a carp. A gloomy thought. Which reminds me—there was one fish in here I respected. He'd been here better than a year when our batch was brought in. He used to skip meals because the boss is cheap enough to resent a glutton. Then every week or so, he'd polish off the smallest fish in the tank. No fooling. We had one poor old night-cleaner accused of trouticide and fired over him.

And he was pretty cute with the customers, too. Whenever someone fingered him and the net started breaking the mirror of the top, he'd turn belly up. That was usually enough to send the customer back to his table, if not out of the place for keeps.

But he grew to rely on it. Stopped using his head. It was funny, really. I could have warned him, if he'd have listened. This big guy with rings under his eyes and a fifty-dollar suit came up to the tank with the manager and the waiter. Now it was obvious from two tables away he was no customer. There was no way a bum like that could afford *our* prices—he could have been wearing his badge on his lapel. You guessed . . . Health Inspector. So our bad actor does his dying flutter and the Inspector whipped him out of there so fast it made your head spin. He ended up *fried* for the bus boys' supper. The management here doesn't waste anything.

Since then I've played it careful. I listen to everything, analysing all the new situations as they come up. You hear some pretty interesting stuff you know, besides the usual table chatter.

For instance, I was the first guy in here to know that the lamprey problem in the Great Lakes had finally been solved. Well, that's a relief, not that it will ever mean anything to me. Like I said, I expect to die in here, peacefully, at night. Unless the place changes hands or burns down.

Am I happy? Sure I am. And don't give me the freedom speeches. Freedom. Most people say it's the chance to look at the sky. Ask yourself, how much sky do you see, when you're a trout?

And think of it another way. From what I hear, things are bad on the streams. From May 1 through September 15, these clowns outside here can angle for you. And they're crafty, don't ever doubt it. What with the new patterns of fly and the Finnish and Japanese artificials these mothers pitch at you, and the new invisible monofilament leaders, life must be murder. Either you have to fast all summer or you become such a selective feeder that you end up neurotic. You have to, because if they catch you —it's for keeps. No, this is the only life for a trout. Except for that one little thing. Yes, it still happens, even after two full seasons in this glass house. It's happening now.

That young man and that girl. He's whispering to her so no one can hear But he needn't trouble, I can lip-read. And he's rubbing his hand over hers. Back and forward, softly, gently. I watch it and my whole median line aches with longing. For those two it's so simple. Just up the stairs to the hotel. So very simple. For me there must be a stream with a current to butt against. There must be rocks and deep places and pools high up away from the lake. There must be the clean scour of gravel. There must be the days of fighting and swimming, bucking the current without resting without feeding until I find that special birth-of-the-world place and fasten myself to it.

There must be freedom, damn you. And all the liver scraps and all the hamburger and all the pride of working in a place with three stars in the guide book—all that counts as nothing.

Oh God, why don't they finish their filthy talk and leave. Or maybe better yet, single *me* out for their honeymoon dinner instead of the inevitable shrimps. Sometimes, you know, sometimes I feel I could throw myself out of this place and die, right down there on the parquet floor.

I'd do it, except that nobody in the whole place would understand why. Can I trust you to tell them?

That Second Cup of Coffee

Marion did not enjoy her ride.

She should have done. It was a perfect morning, sugar-dusted with October frost, and her horse was going well again, the stiffness all worked out of his shoulder. She should have felt happy and the thought worried her as she jogged back, cooling Joker out. She nudged him with her knees and he cantered slowly up the last rise towards the white barn with her red sports car standing in front of it.

She was being silly, she told herself and she pulled herself together, making it physical, a jerk of the head, a stiffening of the spine. This was the American Dream—or as much of it as she had ever coveted. Her own horse, own sports car, money enough for a woman to come in once a week and do the heavy work; what more was there?

She swung down from the saddle and stood arching her back

to relieve the sudden tightness. She took the saddle off Joker and dried his back with a handful of straw. Then she slipped off his bridle and turned him out to run with the other horses in the big paddock where the practice jumps were.

She stood for one happy minute watching him, taking off her hard hat and letting her brown hair spring back to elegant buoyancy.

Her scalp tingled and she frowned. Really, it was an extravagance, having her hair shampooed and set every week when the hard hat pulled it flat within two mornings. Maybe she should quit having it done. It would save five dollars a week. Either that, or quit wearing the hard hat. But Alec wouldn't like that. It would worry him, and that wasn't fair, especially now, when the agency had just changed hands. He had enough to worry about.

The groom came out of the barn, smoking his little black pipe. She turned to walk to her car, stopping to wave and call "Morning Hans, will you put Joker out tomorrow for me, I won't be here." He made a half-circular salute with one finger. "Right, Missis." He didn't stop. The last stable hand would have done, the college boy. He had been very pleasant, a little overpowering perhaps in his maleness, but pleasant. This man was indifferent to people and to horses. He was another of the many people with power to make Marion feel uncomfortable.

For a second she wanted to tell him: "It's Rosemary's birthday tomorrow, I'll have a houseful of nine year olds . . ." but she saved her breath, and her pride.

Instead, she started her car quietly, but backed out to the gate very fast, so that he would know she was busy and had no time to waste.

She drove home at her usual five miles over the limit. Alec's meeting was scheduled for eleven. He would phone her immediately after and she wanted to be there. There was nothing to worry about, Alec had told her, lots of times, too many times perhaps. Sure, the new management had a name for ruthlessness, but then, so did most big corporations when they bought out smaller companies. And besides, he had proved his worth to the company over and over in his twelve years there. Sure, a few people should start worrying, but they would be junior people.

"They'll probably want to cut budgets on us," he had said. "Get rid of some of the aged family retainers that old Brody has kept on out of loyalty. It's easy to understand. They have their cost accounting system to reckon with, there's no room for sentiment in the way they operate."

She had said nothing, just sat smiling and pouring coffee and feeling helpless. It was a jungle down there in the city. Alec didn't stress it much, but he was beginning to look his age. Some of the resiliency was leaving him, although he still kept his interests alive outside the business, his fishing and the garden. But she knew things were not the same between them as they had been ten, or even five years ago.

She swung her car into the driveway of The House. Funny, it would always be The House. The times they had driven past it, in those first years when Brian was just a little boy and Rosemary not even thought of. It had always been "The House" then, the one thing they wanted, the haven.

"One of these days I'm going to make a million dollars and we're going to move in there." Alec had promised. And then it had happened. Not the million dollars part, but they had bought The House, sinking five years of their life into bank payments which had gradually shrunk down to manageable proportions as Alec's salary grew up and up to the money he was making now. So now they had The House. And it needed it's lawn cutting, Marion thought, just once more, before the leaves swept over it and then the snow, to hide everything until next April.

There were letters in the mail box. Bills by the look of them, Marion decided. She flipped through them quickly, guiltily, reading the store names off the envelopes.

Had they really spent money at all those places? It all seemed so pointless; that new blouse of Rosemary's had been laundered twice by now, the books Brian had wanted had been read and would spend the rest of their lives unopened on his shelf. And now the bills were arriving.

She pulled off her boots at the bootjack and padded to the stove in her thick socks, putting the kettle on while she ran upstairs to wash and change.

It was eleven twenty. Alec would be calling soon.

141

She came downstairs, her lipstick freshened, wearing green slacks and a print blouse. The kettle was boiling and she tugged the plug out of the wall deftly while she swung the cupboard door open and reached out the coffee.

She glanced at the clock. Eleven twenty-five. Alec's meeting must be taking longer than the fifteen minutes he had counted on. He had said, "It shouldn't take long. I want raises for two of the juniors. I'll need to show Garfield some samples of the kids' stuff, then listen to a hard luck story about the budget, then accept smaller raises than I ask for." "You have this kind of meeting all the time. What's so special about this one?" She had asked tartly. It was hard to understand what made men so tense over such straightforward things.

He had nodded, slow and calm, reassuring himself. "This is going to be the first time under the new regime. The only man they've really talked to so far is Garfield, the creative director. He's always been a good head. I just want to see how much brainwashing he's absorbed." And then he had kissed her, on the forehead, as if she were a little girl, and left.

She drank her coffee and set to work cleaning the living-room and the immense kitchen. There wasn't much to do, except for the breakfast dishes. Yesterday had been Mrs. Cassidy's day. The place would stay in a state of shell-shocked neatness until the weekend. Then the four of them, and visitors, would build the disorder until Monday brought Mrs. Cassidy's broom and dust-cloth back through the house.

Marion was still a little in awe of her. Other people, friends of Alec's from the office, had wives who talked about the laziness or inefficiency or drinking of their help as if it were all a big joke. Marion couldn't have done that, not about Mrs. Cassidy. Mrs. Cassidy was a silent, grey little Act of God. She gave the impression that money was beneath her. It had to be left out for her, every week, in an envelope. It would have been bad manners to hand her the eight dollars. In a funny way, Marion reflected, Mrs. Cassidy was one of the things that prevented her from enjoying The House as completely as Alec and the children did.

It was after twelve before the dishes were done. Rosemary would be home soon, hungry for lunch and conversation.

Marion opened a can of soup and set it on to heat, then prepared a grated cheese sandwich, with ketchup. Sometimes she would wait until Rosemary came in and then suggest other kinds of lunch, something that took more care in the preparation. But Rosemary would always ask for the same thing. She was easy to please, like her father.

For a moment Marion hated the cheese and soup as symbols of her unchanging routine. She walked to the window. Children were beginning to drift along the street. First the little ones who were let out earliest, then boys, running and throwing. Rosemary would be along soon, walking calmly and steadily with Helga from two doors down.

Two of the boys peeled off from the road and ran onto the front lawn to grab armful of leaves and throw them over one another. Marion smiled. She would have to start burning the leaves soon, before they were thrown or blown all over the lot. The thought pleased her. It was a job that would stay done, for a whole year.

Rosemary came into sight, walking with her friend. They were talking, simultaneously it seemed to Marion. They reached the end of the driveway and split up, still talking, walking backwards away from their parting point until the next house was between them. Then Rosemary turned and walked up the steps. Marion let her in; her cheeks were glowing from the briskness of her walk.

She said, "Hi-i. Lunch ready?"

"Sure is, honey. Just wash up and it'll be on the table." Marion helped her off with her coat, happy to be actively, physically involved. For a moment, she forgot she was waiting to hear from Alec.

Lunch hour was normal. Rosemary kept up a monologue, interrupted by bite-size pauses as she ate her sandwich and drank her soup. Today, one of the grade-sevens had broken his wrist in gym and this afternoon they would have library and Joanne had white net leotards which were hardly neat and the Roberts' had three puppies and why couldn't they have one please Mommy please? because it was going to be her birthday tomorrow and could she please have Joyce Roberts to her party?

The forty minutes flowed by and it was time to help Rosemary back into her coat. Then Helga was at the door and she was gone without a glance back at the house.

Marion waited at the window and as always, Rosemary turned, just as she reached the corner of the lot and they exchanged waves, a quick, warm hug of a signal.

The house was quiet. It was one o'clock.

The phone rang, jarring her so urgently that she shuddered. She ran to it. "Hello."

Alec's voice was even, controlled. "Marion?"

"What's the matter?"

"I'm . . . I'm leaving this place. I don't want to discuss it on the phone. Right now I'm going for a beer. Then I'll come home."

"Fine." Marion felt she had to add something. "I'll be burning the leaves."

"Good. I'll help you."

There was a pause, heavy with unasked questions. It stretched on until the tension was too much and Marion heard the slow click as Alec hung up without saying anything more.

She did the same, replacing the white receiver slowly as if it were very, very heavy.

Alec was going to leave his job.

She was surprised to find how calm the news left her. He never did anything without good reason. He would tell her the reason when he came in.

Anyway, she had things to do if he were coming home early. She turned to the table and began to clear away, moving quietly, thoughtlessly, in a way that would have reminded her of Mrs. Cassidy had she been able to see herself.

It was a little after three when Alec arrived home. Marion was raking the leaves, feeding twin dragons of fire, one on each frosted flowerbed. Her face was flushed and the wind had teased her hair forward out from beneath the kerchief she was wearing.

He stopped his Camaro opposite her and got out, slowly straightening to his full six feet.

"They fired me," he said.

"You're kidding." It started as a whisper but ran up into a cry.

144

"No I'm not." He managed a crooked grin. "To use their own language, they weren't exactly fascist about it. They've given me three months severance pay."

"How much does that work out to?"

"Enough to feed a starving Chinese family for twenty-two years," Alec said testily.

"I'm sorry."

He came over to her and put his arm around her shoulder. His breath smelled of beer. She put up her mouth to be kissed. "I didn't mean to snap," he said.

They kissed hungrily as if he had been away for a long time; a wartime kiss.

Then Alec released her. He was grinning again.

"Why don't you put that rake down and come inside."

She dropped the rake and let out a little gasp of laughter. "I was holding it right in your back."

Alec grinned a little wider, a little too wide. "I know, and there's a knife in there already."

He put his arm around her again and they walked up the steps to the door.

In the kitchen, Marion looked at him, sharply. "You want Instant?"

"Whatever you like." Alec shrugged and sat down slowly in the breakfast nook. He looked tired.

Marion said nothing while the water boiled. She got out the mugs and spoons and jars, trying to keep her mind filled with the little task. When the coffee was made, she handed Alec a mug and asked, "What did they say, exactly?"

"They said thanks." Alec sipped his coffee and set it down. "It wasn't really a 'they' anyway. It was Malloy. He's been brought in as general manager for a year. He's a head office man really, he does the hatchet work for them wherever they take over." He paused again and Marion waited, swallowing her impatience. He went on, leaning forward to stare down into his coffee cup. "I told you I'd been waiting to see Garfield, the creative director. Well, he didn't come in this morning. And then the next thing I know, Malloy calls for me and starts showing me his budget sheets. He's sixty thousand a year over budget on creative salaries." Alec snorted, a quick little har-

145

umph of bottled laughter. "I still didn't hear the alarm bells ringing."

Marion said, "Are they . . . are they letting a lot of people go?"

Now Alec looked up at her, his blue eyes wide in emphasis. "Seven of us. Seven out of twenty-four."

He stood up and walked over to the window, his hands jammed into his pockets, elbows thrust forward like a guilty schoolboy. Marion noticed how thin his hair was becoming at the back. He turned around quickly, as if trying to catch her staring at him. "Guess who the first casualty is?"

"You?"

"No, I'm the second. First of all they're getting rid of Garfield."

"But he's the creative director."

"He's been the entire creative department in his time. Now they've got a new group upstairs and its a 'what-have-you-done-for-us today?' kind of attitude."

"Did Malloy tell you that, about Garfield I mean?"

"Yes. They're offering him the creative director's job in Montreal. He'd be a fool to take it. It's a demotion, and Lord knows, they'd fire him tomorrow if they decided to. These guys don't have any loyalty."

"Listen." Marion held up her hands, quickly, in a way she hadn't done since she quit teaching kindergarten to become Mrs. Alec Hansen. "That's all over now. What they're doing to you, or to anybody else, has stopped being important. Now it's our turn to act."

"You're right." Alec came back from the window and sat down, quietly. "My severance pay will work out to around five thousand dollars, after tax."

Marion said, "That was more than you earned in a year when we were first married."

"I know, but we weren't living here then."

Marion smiled, a slow smile that let her eyes droop closed so that she could remember.

That first apartment—if you could call a room on one floor and a kitchen downstairs an apartment. They had stayed on in it, even after Alec left college and took that first job with the newspaper. They had even managed to save on his eighty dollars a week. True, the car they bought had been junked ten years now, and the baby clothes she had bought for Brian had long ago been sent away in some goodwill bag or other. They had nothing to show for that first year of marriage and work, nothing except a sixteen-year-old son.

"Penny for 'em." Alec almost snapped it.

"I was thinking of Allister Avenue, that awful brown lino in the kitchen . . . ."

"And that low room divider," Alec grinned. "I'd still have a full head of hair if it hadn't been for that thing. The times I dinged my head . . . ."

"And the squirrels. Remember that black one who used to roll over on his back."

It was becoming too painful.

Alec said, "Well, we could always start out all over again. I guess there are still squirrels up on Allister."

Marion made her first sacrifice, turning away from the past, being practical, level-headed.

"You're not going to do anything today, promise me."

"Well, I did think of calling up Harper and Lewis, they need a writer, but they've got a lousy reputation."

He stood up and walked over to the phone, but indecisively.

Marion moved between him and the receiver. "Don't. Not today, you're still up in the air."

Alec nodded blindly and sat down again. "It's so damned unfair. They *do* have people around there who aren't worth their salt. I could name six of them. But they're not being fired." He rammed his fingers through his hair and over his head and down to his collar. "It's not a good time of year to be looking for a job. Around now everybody is putting in time till Christmas for their bonus. I don't know where to start."

Marion made herself a second cup of coffee. Then she said, "Well, I think I do." She softened it for him when she saw the surprise in his eyes. "I read something somewhere, some magazine at the orthodontist's while I was waiting for Rosemary."

"I'm all agog," Alec said, and the brightness wasn't forced this time.

"We start by making a list of how much we pay out per month and to whom."

"Sounds sensible, but like I said, I've got five grand coming to me."

"Swell. Because we've got about forty dollars in the bank, and that's all."

Marion pulled open the kitchen drawer and took out her shopping pad and pencil.

"Let's see now. Standing expenses. First off, there's the mortgage."

"Right. Put down a hundred and seventy bucks," Alec said.

Marion wrote *Mortgage* in a tight little script, then skipped across the page and set down *$170* in the same neat banker's hand.

"Then there's the car payments."

Marion nodded and wrote. "And your insurance."

They listed the expenses—phone, heat, electricity and Marion felt her anxiety beginning to rise. Why wasn't he mentioning her horse? Seventy dollars a month it cost them. That was twice the heat or electricity bill.

Alec said, "Well, that just about wraps it up, doesn't it." She could read the truth in his face. He had thought about the horse, about the credit card for her sports car and the charge accounts at the two stores downtown. He had thought about them and he was not going to mention them. He was afraid. She felt her voice becoming brittle.

"There's a whole lot more, you know that."

Alec stared at her with extravagant blankness. "Like what?"

"Like horse board, seventy dollars." She found herself pressing on her pencil, writing bigger. "Like forty dollars a month to Jackman's and another thirty to Meyer's. And then there's twenty a month for the credit card for my car. And the insurance is due next month."

She added these totals separately and looked up at him defiantly. "That's just about two hundred dollars a month for nothing."

"Oh come on now, dear . . . ." His face made her ashamed of what she had done. It wasn't fair to punish him like this.

"But it's true," she said helplessly.

Alec sat very still for a moment, staring at a tiny coffee stain on the table cloth.

"It's not true." His voice was so soft she could hardly make out the words.

148

"But dear, two hundred dollars a month . . . ." She spread her arms.

"It's not true." He shook his head very deliberately. "That's the trouble with the scene I've been through this morning. People think that figures are the truth. So long as you can count it up and draw a line underneath it and write a total down, that's the truth. That's what they think at the office. And they're wrong. All that matters is people. Not money."

His voice dropped away and for a long moment, Marion thought he was going to cry.

She ached to put her arms around him, to rock him against her but something deep and tough and primitive told her it would be the wrong thing to do, now.

She looked down at her paper, counting the total, slowly and carefully checking each of the figures and then totting them twice. The total came to a few dollars less than a thousand.

"That's nine hundred and seventy three a month."

Alec looked at her calmly now.

"You included grocery money, and something for me every week to drive downtown, job hunting?"

She nodded. He laughed a quick humourless snort. "If that's all it comes to, how in thunder have we been getting overdrawn every month?"

"Easy." Marion felt suddenly pleased with her knowledge and control. "These are just the standing still expenses. There's nothing in here for clothes for the kids, holidays, presents, parties, dentists, all the extras."

"I see." Alec sat still for a moment and Marion guessed he was adding the total of books, records, theatre tickets and liquor that he bought so casually in any month. He said. "I guess I get through eighty bucks a month in extras, on my own."

"It's not difficult," she said primly. "Now then. How much severance pay did you say you had coming?"

"Five thousand, if they tax me the way I expect. Which means we can manage for five months."

"Better than that." Marion tore the first page neatly from the pad and began writing on the second. She was flattered to hear Alec's chuckle.

"Have you been taking book-keeping lessons on the sly?"

149

"I told you, I read an article at the orthodontist's."

"Kind of makes you glad young Rosemary's got buck teeth," Alec said.

There had been no article. Marion had stored every fact she had come across through years of worrying what would happen if the bubble should burst. Now she was ready, and she smiled.

"There are some things you can put off for a month or two."

"Like for instance . . . ?" His voice only a little mocking.

"Like for instance your car payments. You can pay just the interest for two months in any year."

She made a quick calculation and wrote *Save $110.00 (?)* on the fresh sheet.

Alec said, "Then there's my investment club. I can suspend that until I get something definite."

"Right." She wrote *$75.00* on her sheet.

"Anything else? The rest of the things are pretty permanent aren't they?"

He was asking *her* advice. Marion could have wept.

"Most of them. But we can postpone payments on the charge accounts, if we write and let them know what's happened."

"Do we want to do that?" He was frowning again.

"Well, it's the truth, after all, and it'll save us seventy dollars a month."

"Fair enough." He nodded, pursed-mouthed, reluctant but yielding.

"And then there's the mortgage. We don't have to do it right away, but if you don't get settled inside a month or two, we can pay them just the interest."

"God, I intend to be settled before then."

"You will be." She did not hold on to her own little triumph, not over his anxiety. "Of course you will be. I'm just saying what we could do."

"Fine. Only we're not going to need it. Tomorrow I start knocking on doors. Right now I'm going to get my sample book into shape."

He got up, without looking in her direction and walked away upstairs. She listened to his footsteps leading up and back to the study at the rear of the house. It was the place he worked when he stayed home on crash programmes. It held a desk and a

150

typewriter and his file cabinet, full of proofs and tear sheets of advertisements he had written, and tapes and films of his commercials. He had joked about them in the past, calling himself a pack rat to store so much old paperwork but he had never thrown any out. In his own way he had been protecting himself against today. Now he would put together his presentation book and start making the rounds. Marion knew he would find another job. It might take time, months perhaps, but the fabric of the advertising community was woven loosely. As soon as people moved, others moved in to fill their places, leaving other places behind them. Some opening would show up somewhere, sometime. And in the meantime . . . . Marion sat with her coffee cup and the pieces of notepaper. The neatness of the figures charmed her. She picked the papers up and read them over, as objectively as if they were an arithmetic exercise she was marking.

Even if Alec didn't find a job, they could manage on this money for close to a year. And long before that time they could sell this big house and move into an apartment. She could get rid of the horse and her car and even go back to work again.

When you really stopped to look at it, there were so many things she could do to help.

For the first time in years, there was nothing to worry about. She looked down at the last inch of her coffee and then drank it, happy to find as always that it was the sweetest part of the cup. Then she slowly put the empty cup into the sink and walked upstairs to find Alec, her heart full to tears with a slow, warm happiness.

American Primitive

Nobody saw him coming into town.

Later, when the news was in all the papers, a lot of people claimed to have seen him.

But none of them had. Not unless they were drivers on a City garbage truck. The garbage men saw him, up at the city dump. Because that's where he lived.

He built himself a shack out of crates, dressed himself up in two pairs of pants and a kid's ski jacket he found up there, and ate whatever he could get. Not that he ever seemed hungry. He was always too busy, sorting the garbage, picking it over. He used to keep on sorting even after the sun went down, working by the light of the fires that burn all the time at the dump.

Some of the truckdrivers used to drop him off a sandwich or something out of their lunch sometimes; or maybe some food they had picked up at a restaurant somewhere. A loaf of bread that wasn't more than a few days old, bits of leftover meat loaf.

They said he never thanked them. Never used to say anything, come to that.

Someone persevered long enough once to find out that his name was Carl. So then people took to calling him Crazy Carl. He didn't care. All he was interested in was sorting out the garbage and stacking it.

He had three stacks. In one of them he had bottles. Maybe a hundred-dollars worth of bottles that people had been too lazy to send back to the store. In another stack he had all kinds of iron. A truck motor at the bottom and a pile of tin cans and old appliances.

The third stack was concrete, blocks and pieces of Redi-mix that had been dumped out and had hardened.

Nobody bothered with him. Living at the dump, with all those rats, he was left to himself. He worked all through the winter. The cold didn't seem to stop him and he didn't get sick. And then it was spring, and Easter came. Naturally enough the City employees got the holiday. So there was nobody up at the dump for three whole days.

Crazy Carl must have worked all that time, all seventy-two hours to complete what he did. The first truckdriver to come in, around noon on the Monday, was amazed by what he saw. Carl had built his garbage up into three towers. Not just heaps, but real towers.

One of the towers was made all of bottles, stacked neck to neck and base to base in a solid column of glass three feet through, braced around with chicken wire.

The second tower was all iron. It took off from the truck engine and rose up in a tangle of tin cans and rusting appliances cases.

The third tower was the grandest. It was all the bits of concrete. Carl must have worked like a madman to get some blocks up the side of that tower. He was only a tiny man, the boy's snow jacket was big on him, yet there were stones up near the top that weighed a hundred, maybe two hundred pounds.

And there the three towers stood, right in the middle of the smoke and smell of the garbage dump. Taller than a house, all the same size, arranged in a perfect triangle. They were beauti-

154

ful, in a weird way. Made you feel quiet inside. The trucker and his helper stopped and looked for a while. Then they noticed that Carl wasn't picking around like he usually did. So after a bit of debating they went over to his shack and opened up the flap of sacking he had across the front and looked in.

Carl was there. So were a lot of rats.

There was nothing the men could do right then. So they called their office on the nearest phone and told them about old Crazy Carl being dead. Then the police came up, and a man from the newspaper.

And that was when all the excitement started.

Carl was almost forgotten in the fuss over his towers. The art critic from the City paper came up and looked at them. And he brought up an engineer and a photographer. And pretty soon the Mayor was there, getting his picture taken in front of those three strange columns.

People came and went all day. The art critic wrote a feature entitled "A poor man's monument" in which he compared the piles with Stonehenge and two different sets of pyramids. He said that it was tragic that the man's primitive, forceful talents had not been acknowledged in his lifetime. He had died unrecognized, a Gauguin of the garbage mounds.

The engineer measured them. He calculated that the towers were each exactly the same height: $42'\,3\frac{7}{16}''$. He also said that this was a remarkable feat of engineering for a man, working barehanded with a pile of ill-assorted junk.

The poor, gnawed husk that had been Crazy Carl, the hermit, the sculptor, was taken to the city morgue. The coroner signed a death certificate stating the cause of death to have been malnutrition—which didn't seem to make sense when you thought of the work he must have done, but the coroner was firm about it. After that, the body should have been sent to the nearest medical school, the usual routine for unclaimed cadavers. But some citizen, signing himself "Art Lover," delivered an envelope containing two thousand dollars to the morgue and requested cremation of the remains.

All this took place in the afternoon. At nightfall the trouble started.

A crowd of rowdies rode into town on their motorcycles. The

punks for miles around, come to sneer at Carl's monument. For an hour or two the police tried to chase them off, but finally the order came from the Mayor: Forget it. What sense was there in some policeman getting injured protecting three piles of garbage?

There was public outcry when this announcement was broadcast over the radio. Art lovers from hundreds of miles away phoned to offer to pay for the protection of the towers until they could be moved to a permanent site. But that night there was nothing to stop all those bullies in their leather jackets and chrome-plated German helmets. They swarmed over the piles, stamping through the fires in their high boots, drinking cheap wine, shouting and swearing. Even the garbage dump seemed too civilized a spot for their activities.

By now it was dark and it was hard for them to find stones to throw at the glass tower. But as soon as the first wine bottle was empty, someone hurled it against the stacked glass and the splintering crash mingled with the wolfish howls of glee.

Neither sound was audible aboard the saucer-shaped craft which rode upon the pull of Earth's gravity, fifty-eight miles above the towers.

Only a flicker of imbalance on the face of the Mass Perceptor indicated some deviation in the message they were receiving. The crewman at the controls reported the fact to the Master of the craft.

The Master inquired whether the balances were still within their projected limits: did the trinitower still project a trivik of values, one to eight to fourteen, accurate to six coanes of biax?

The crewman responded affirmatively.

And so the Master ordered the motors started again. Gently he followed his flight path down and down until the triple receivers on the underside of his ship rested elegantly on the tips of the towers. And then, following the final instruction of the pioneer Kull who had built the spaceport, he seared and sterilized the entire area with one flash of brilliant, purifying heat.

Dependents

She was standing at the window when they entered the room, her hands at her sides, her eyes fixed on a point beyond their view, out in the snow-covered yard. She did not look around but called "Hello," and then, "Boys, come quickly."

David and Arthur ran to her, crackling over yesterday's newspaper scattered about the floor. Their grandmother laid her hands on their shoulders and said, "See, the green birds, they're evening grosbeaks."

David, who was eleven, said, "Grosbeaks? I never heard of them before," and his younger brother said, "Boy. They got real clunky looking mouths."

Behind the three of them, Murray and his wife exchanged glances. Helen, still in her coat and gloves, stooped automatically to pick up the scattered sheets of newspaper. Frank Murray bent to help her, grunting at the unaccustomed exertion.

159

His mother was answering the boys. To David she said, "Grosbeaks are shy. They usually live in pine woods. You never see them unless you have a feeding station."

Murray wondered, as he stooped, if the remark were a reproach for the fact that he was bringing up his boys in an eighth floor apartment instead of a house.

His mother went on, to Arthur, "Grosbeak means big beak. They have a big beak because they live on seeds. They use their beaks like nutcrackers." Arthur said "Hey, neat."

Murray advanced to his mother's side and kissed her cheek. Her skin was cool and gathered, like the skin of a russet apple, smelling of violets. She patted his face with her frail old kitten-paw hand. "Hello, dear."

He said "How are you, Mom?" wishing she would turn away from the window, feeling ridiculous with his hands full of crumpled paper.

Outside, on the rough wooden tray he had hung for her in the apple tree, the dusty, businesslike grosbeaks started upright and flew off to the end of the yard.

Now his mother turned away. "They're such polite feeders," she said. "They just take what they need and go away till the next day. Not like sparrows." She advanced to her daughter-in-law, moving with firm little steps. "Helen dear, how are you?"

They kissed, affectionately, on the lips. The old lady said, "You picked up the paper. Thank you. I was going to and then I had visitors."

Murray crumpled up his pieces of paper and took Helen's from her. "Visitors? One of the neighbours drop in?"

His mother laughed quickly and waved one hand in apology for misleading him. "My grosbeaks. They visit me every day. I love to see them but they don't stay any time to speak of. I just drop whatever I'm doing and watch them."

Murray gave a quick glance around the dusty room and thought that perhaps the birds came more often than she realized.

He said, "Well, you've got two kinds of visitors today. Now we're here."

"And it's lovely to see you. I'll just put the kettle on."

Helen asked "Can I help you?" but the old lady shook her head. "No thank you, dear. Sit down, I'll only be a moment."

She filled the kettle and turned on the gas stove with a little plop. Murray crunched his newspaper as small as it would go and stuffed it into the kitchen garbage container. It filled it so full that the lid wouldn't close and he asked his mother, "Where d'you keep the garbage bags?"

"In the bottom drawer." She indicated with the spoon from the tea caddy. "But don't put the newspaper in there, I always put it out separately and then they can recycle it."

Helen gave an astonished little laugh. "Recycle it? Mother, you're a wonder."

The old lady frowned. "Mrs. Graham was explaining it to me. If they use the paper over again it saves trees." She paused to look around, her lips moving as she counted them and put an appropriate number of spoons of tea into the pot. "I think it's good that they're trying to save trees."

Murray said, "The grosbeaks have to have some place to live, right?"

His tone was joking but she answered seriously. "That's right."

The boys had wandered into the kitchen, ill at ease and bored.

She turned to them. "Would you boys like a cookie?"

When they said they would, she took out the tin of cookies that had been one of their presents to her at Christmas and put some out on a plate. Murray watched her, pleased to see how capably she moved. You would never realize she was seventy-eight. She kept herself alert and sharp. It was a big relief. He listened as she and Helen chatted about the boys. David's hockey and Arthur's baby teeth.

When the tea was poured at last, golden in the thin porcelain of her best cups, he told her the news.

"You're coming on holiday with us."

He found he was addressing the side of her head as she swivelled in her chair to look out at the feeding station.

"Well I'll be . . . ." She was angry suddenly, her colour rising, her lips pursed so that the fine hairs on her upper lip glinted in the bright reflection from the snow outside.

"What's the matter?" Murray stood up and went to the window. She was there beside him, moving almost as quickly as he did.

"Look. He's back." She pointed indignantly out at the feeding tray, swinging now under the weight of a ginger and white cat that crouched there gnawing at the bread crusts. "Look at that." Her voice had the firmness of a woman half her age. "He gets here every day at this time. I swear they never feed him."

"Where's he from?" Murray asked. And does it matter? he thought. We're about to take you south out of the snow and you're worrying about a stray cat. He kept his temper and listened to her patient answer.

"I think it comes from the next street. It always comes through Mrs. Graham's and under the fence. But it's not hers."

Murray took her by the shoulder. "Well, it'll go away in a minute, come drink your tea."

She shook her shoulder peevishly. "It won't. It will eat all the bread and then it will sit there and I won't have any more visitors all day."

Helen had joined them, and they all stood and looked out at the ginger cat, a coil of appetite filling the tray, oblivious to the cold, the birds that piped from the remote branches of the tree, the hatred directed at it from the kitchen window.

Helen had the first idea. "David, Arthur. Go and put your boots on and chase that cat away from Nana's bird feeder."

David said "Sure, Mom," and with a hint of his father's authority in his voice, "C'm'on Arthur."

They thumped down the couple of steps to the back door, tumbling against one another in their eagerness.

Murray called to them. "David, take the keys and get your hockey stick out of the trunk. Give him a whack with that."

Conversation at the window stopped while the boys whooped into the yard and banged at the feeding tray. The cat glared down at them then gave an easy hop into the crotch of the tree, beyond the reach of the stick.

David began to climb up, slipping once then finding a purchase and pulling himself into the branches. He reached back down for the hockey stick that Arthur handed to him, poised on tiptoe. Then, working his way up the trunk he drove the cat into the topmost branches.

At this point Helen banged on the kitchen window and signalled for him to come down. Murray was glad she had done it, not wanting to be the first to show fear for his son's safety. "A pity he can't reach it, that would scare it away for good. He swings a mean hockey stick."

Impulsively he turned and trotted down the steps and into the yard to help his son down from the tree and climb it himself.

The cat hissed at him but deferred to his reach and jumped nimbly down and ran under the fence into the yard behind. Murray dropped down again, panting and handed the stick back to David. "Thanks son. Stay out here a minute or two and whip a snowball at it if it comes back."

David said "Hey, yeah," his eyes gleaming with the ferocity of innocence. "C'm'on Arthur, let's make a pile of snowballs." He dropped the hockey stick and Murray picked it up with the complaint unspoken on his lips: That stick cost three dollars. I never had a new stick at your age. Instead he carried it back into the house and propped it inside the back door. His wife and mother were still standing at the window. Helen was saying "We're going to drive down, nice and easy, none of those six-hundred-mile days that Frank used to go in for when we were first married."

Murray took up his corner of the banter. It was his duty, this was his mother and he was the dutiful son. "Never mind the poormouth when I'm out cat-hunting. I'm the slowest driver ever to make the Florida run." He came up the three little steps into the kitchen, feeling suddenly as if thirty years had dropped from his age and he was a teenager again, coming home to silent disapproval for some unkindness.

His mother was saying, "You're so kind, both of you, so very good to me."

But . . . Murray thought, it's coming up the very next word. "But I just couldn't go."

"Why on earth not?" Helen's voice crackled with impatience. "Two weeks in the sun would be great. By the time you get back, winter will be about over."

"I just couldn't go." The old lady was shaking her head firmly, her years slipping away until it seemed she was not querulous, merely haughty. She was smiling but it was a formal smile that did not take away any of the sharpness of her refusal.

Murray felt his frustration starting again, as it had when he had talked Helen into suggesting this sacrifice. Now it was being thrown back at him and he was doubly humiliated. He almost blushed.

"What's to stop you going?" he asked it very calmly, the engineer analysing the logistics.

"There would be nobody here to attend to the bird table."

Murray made the word a joke, emphasizing the syllable and letting the others dangle. "The *bird* table."

Helen was kinder. "Surely you could get somebody to throw them some bread every day. Mrs. Graham would do it."

The old lady set down her cup and touched Helen's wrist. "I think my Frank is a very lucky man to have met you, Helen, you're quite prepared to take me along on your vacation and that's lovely of you."

"I'm a queen," Helen said tartly. Then, to minimize the sharpness she put one finger under her chin and mimed a little curtsy. Her mother-in-law smiled again, another formality, and gave her another playful pat on the wrist.

Murray took over. "Why can't somebody else feed them? They're only birds."

"I know they're only birds. That's what makes it important to keep on the way they're used to. They come to see me and my feeding station is all they know. They would die if I wasn't here." Her tone had become very forceful, almost angry and she brought herself down from her intensity by shaking her head and saying, "My dears, you don't just throw them some bread."

Murray shrugged. "Bread, bird seed, what does it matter, someone will do it."

His mother became his mother again, taking his hand and turning him away from her, back to the table. "Your tea's getting cold," she said.

He did not move for a moment, but stood staring over her head at his wife until he realized that his action had all of the petulance he would have expected from his younger son. Then he laughed, and turned back to the table.

"Now I've heard everything," he said. "You're giving up a couple of weeks sunshine for the sake of a bunch of grosbeaks."

Why didn't she protest? Why didn't she tell him that she

164

knew they didn't really want her with them? Why this nonsense about birds?

She said, "I appreciate the offer very much, both of you. I know how much it means to share your vacation with another person."

"You're not—another person—you're the boys' grandmother," Helen said. Also a baby-sitter, Murray thought. But of course, she realizes that.

He swallowed the last of his tea, angrily. "Dammit Mother, what does it take to please you?"

"Not very much," she said. Somehow she seemed to have dwindled during the conversation so that she was elegantly frail and vulnerable like one of her rare birds. She fluttered with the tea things, pouring more tea for each of them. "Now that you ask me, there is something."

"What is it?" The question burst from Murray's mouth and from his wife's simultaneously.

The old lady said, "You're supposed to shake little fingers and say 'bread and butter' when you do that."

Such was their guilt that they did it.

She nodded approvingly. "I want two things. First, I want to get rid of that cat. What do you suggest?"

Murray turned his methodical mind to the subject, firing out suggestions as rapidly as one of his computer programmes spitting out figures. He mentioned the Humane Society, traps, a cat-proof feeding station, although that would have to wait until spring. Finally he said, "I could always get you a pellet gun."

His mother laughed, a tinkling young laugh that heartened all three of them.

"Really, Frank. I could never use a gun."

Murray realized how intense his eagerness had been and hammed a little to release the tension. "You'd be keepin' society free for decent folks and their feathered friends," he drawled.

It was Helen who offered the answer. "It comes for the food. You could always feed it a little at the back door. That would keep it away from the birds."

The old lady nodded, her eyes wide with a respect Murray had never before seen there. "What a good idea. That's the answer, Helen. I must remember right now." She left the table, seeming not to notice the glance they exchanged, went to the message pad beside her telephone and wrote "Cat food" on her shopping list, enunciating the words carefully as she wrote.

Murray picked up the success and swept her before them with it. "So that's problem number one out of the way. What's the other thing?"

The old lady pursed her lips and nodded thoughtfully. "Well, it's a bit harder," she said.

Murray listened and waited, stilling the urge to tell her to give him the request. He would answer it for her. He could afford to. She explained, while he kept his peace.

"Well, I have a bit of trouble putting food on the table."

"The *bird* table?" Helen suggested, wondering from the phrasing whether her mother-in-law was going hungry.

The old lady nodded again. "That's right. I have to stand on something to put it up there. And some days it's kind of slippery."

Murray said, "Stand on something? You don't mean to say you drag the stepladder out there every time you put feed out."

"Oh no." She dismissed the suggestion with an amused wave. "No, of course not, dear. I just take a kitchen chair."

Murray contained his horror. His mind ran the silent film through his head at enormous speed. The tipped chair, the broken hip, the agonizing wait in the snow until some neighbour noticed from a rear window.

"Don't do that, mother," he said solemnly. "Don't ever do that."

"Now, now. I'm not one of your boys, I'm careful," she said.

She knows what I'm thinking, Murray thought. I don't have to spell it out.

"Well, don't do it," he said again.

"I don't want to," she said impishly. "The chair is getting heavier and heavier to carry."

Murray felt compelled to go and kiss her on the cheek again. A reward, as if for a child showing particular cleverness.

"I'll build you a permanent ladder," he said.

But she was shaking her head. "I thought of that. But if I left

166

anything there the cats would get up it so easily I'd never have any birds."

"O.K." Murray turned away and looked out of the window at the feeding table full of chicadees and juncos, jostling for the seed.

"Then we need a portable feeding-station filler," he announced. "And I have the very idea."

He went back down the steps to the rear door and out to the car, opening the trunk and taking out the roll of tape from his son's hockey bag. Then he came back into the house, laughing a protest at the snowballs his sons hit him with. He took up the hockey stick from beside the door and went over to the garbage. There was a soup can lying there. He picked it out and stripped the label from it. His mother watched him, interested almost in spite of her problem.

"What are you doing, Frank?" He said nothing, just winked at her and proceeded to tape the empty can to the blade of the hockey stick, close to the tip. When it was firmly in place he held it out to her. "See. The patented Murray bird-feed dispenser. Fill the can, tilt the stick and pour it onto the feeding station, four feet above your head."

Her face glowed with delight and appreciation. "Isn't that clever," she said. She accepted the hockey stick as if it were a sceptre. "Look at that, Helen. Look at what your clever husband has made."

Helen said, "Yes, he does have his moments."

The old lady held up the stick and gave it a couple of little jogging motions as if emptying the contents into an imaginary feeding tray. "Yes," she said firmly. "That will work just fine. Just fine."

The boys barged in through the back door, faces red from the cold, noisy, cheerful. Their grandmother showed them the stick, even before they had their overboots off. "Look what your Daddy made me to feed my birds with."

They both looked, suspended in their kicking off of overshoes, one foot on the ground, one foot swinging, one hand on the wall. Little Arthur said, "Will they really eat out of the can?" David said, "Hey, Nana, that's my good stick."

His father said "I'll get you another one, remind me, on the way home." David's face was very straight, he was not going to cry. "I like that one," he said, in a quiet voice.

Murray began to speak, "I'll get you another one, with a curved blade, just the same."

The boy said nothing, just went on kicking off his overshoe, not looking at any of them. His mother said, "How be if we bring Nana another one next week and get this one back."

He looked up now, but not in agreement, only bright-eyed with the chance to have them see things his way. "But I have a game in the morning," he said. "That's my good stick. I got a goal with it, and an assist."

"Then why did you leave it outside . . . ." Murray began angrily.

His mother held up her hand to quiet them. "Let Davie take his stick. If you feed the birds tonight for me, I'll manage tomorrow and I'll get Mrs. Graham to get an old stick off her grandson. He lives just around the block."

David looked at his father, guiltily, waiting for approval.

Murray bit back his annoyance. Why couldn't anyone let anyone do anyone a favour around here? Without speaking he borrowed a kitchen knife and cut the tape from the stick. He set the can down on the kitchen table, along with the hockey tape. "You know how to tape one on then, Mother."

She nodded her head, calmingly. "Sure, dear, thank you."

David realized he was not going to be excused easily. He said, "I'm sorry, Nana. It's my real good stick."

The old lady said, "I know, Davie. Don't worry about it."

Murray watched as she patted the boy's head. He was angry at his own feeling of guilt. Dammit. Dammit. Why did they come around here anyway? She always ended up making him feel like a heel.

There seemed very little to say and soon the boys put their boots back on and Helen washed the tea things and they left.

The old lady watched and waved from the kitchen window. Then turned to look out at the feeding station. The ginger cat was coming back, creeping on its belly across the snow, stalking the reckless sparrows in the tree.

Quickly she turned and opened the refrigerator. There was

milk left in the pitcher she had put out for the tea. She emptied it into a saucer and took it to the back door. She stood there, holding the saucer and calling to the cat. The growing chill of late afternoon bit through her blouse, making her shudder, slightly at first and then vigorously. Despite the cold she stood there until the cat came up to her. It stood on its hind legs and sniffed at the saucer. The old lady said "Good kitty. Pretty kitty." She lowered the saucer until the cat could reach to drink. Then, moving with surprising speed, she caught up the cat by the back of the neck and lifted it into the house. She set it and the saucer down and closed the door. The cat crouched over the milk, lapping with a purring, mechanical precision. The old lady looked on and smiled. "Got you," she whispered sweetly.

Susan

It was after six when Paul Wheatley pulled his Toronado up beside the diner. Through the window he could see that his daughter, Susan, wasn't ready to leave, although another girl had come on duty. Time was one of the abstract ideas that Susan's limited intelligence would never be able to handle.

Paul shut off the engine and unfolded his length from the driver's seat, thankful that the diner was practically empty.

Susan was wiping a table at the far end of the room when he entered, her back towards him, her whole body wagging in a puppylike earnestness. Paul sensed her expression: eyebrows bunched together in a frown, mouth slightly open with the tip of her tongue showing at one corner. With people in Susan's category, every chore was a matter for fierce concentration. He looked at her and loved her so much it hurt him.

The other girl said, "Hi, Mr. Wheatley."

171

"Hi, Mary," Paul replied, nodding towards Susan, "how're we doing?"

"Hard worker," said the waitress and smiled. She knows there's no competition, Paul thought. She can afford to be generous.

Susan turned to him then, her blue eyes wide with surprise: "Gee, Dad, 'it that time a'ready." There it was, the unmistakable shapelessness of her words, a sloughing off of the harder sounds. He would probably never learn to stop worrying about them.

"Sure is, kitten," Paul said, thinking she's seventeen now, getting too old for a ponytail. He watched her walk to the other side of the counter and call a goodnight to the proprietor back somewhere in the kitchen. And then a boy who had been sitting in the corner booth got up and moved towards the door. He was short, compactly built, his hair blond and crisp, and he was dressed in green work pants and a checkered shirt.

"Dad," Susan said, "this is Jimmy Drew. He's asked me to go dancing with him tonight."

Paul said "That's lovely" and hoped his face concealed the shock of knowing the time had come, the moment he had dreaded for twelve years, ever since that final I.Q. test had pegged down Susan's future. Her first date.

He held out his hand to the boy and said, "Hi, Jimmy."

The boy shook his hand, quickly, like a prize-fighter. "Hi, Mister Wheatley. Nice to meet you."

The complete poker face, Paul thought. I wonder who he is and where he comes from, and why he has to pick on us when he has so many other people to choose from. He said, "We'll see you later, then, Jimmy."

"Yeah," said the boy. "Be seein' you, Susan," and walked back to his seat in the corner.

Susan said 'G'night.' Paul nodded to the boy. Apparently the formalities had been fulfilled, he decided, although he couldn't help feeling cheated. He ushered Susan out and opened the car door for her. Neither of them spoke until the car had started. Paul asked as casually as he could "Where are you going with Jim?"

Susan was lying back, her eyes focused beyond the fleeting scenery on either side of the car.

172

"With Jim?" she echoed. "Oh, you mean Jimmy. Oh, we're going to the dance over Claremont."

Eleven miles from home, Paul registered—a long way for a first date, especially for Susan. He began to whistle silently, weighing his next words. He chose: "Seems like a nice boy, does he go to school?"

"School!" Susan shrilled. "He helps on the pop truck," and Paul grinned wryly as he realised how his wife would take this information. Susan was looking at him, her face revealing the struggle that was going on within the confused corridors of her brain.

"Dad," she said at last, "you won't let Kay laugh at me, will you?"

Paul took one hand from the wheel and squeezed her shoulder, very tight.

"Just leave it to me, Susie," he said, with a confidence he did not feel.

He found his wife in the kitchen putting the crowning flourish to a salad. Paul kissed her cheek. She put her hand on his shoulder in a gesture that was half embrace, half restraint. Paul said, "Met a friend of Susan's when I picked her up from work tonight." He was glad Susan had gone upstairs and did not hear Alice's sigh.

"Must you say 'work,' dear. Heaven knows we don't *need* the wretched twenty-eight dollars."

Paul lifted a celery stick from the dish. "You can call it therapy when you're with your bridge club. For simplicity's sake, I'm going to call it 'work'."

"All right, Paul." Her voice was tired, but Paul excused her. Every day of her daughter's life had brought her more concern than the average woman would ever know.

"This girl, is she nice?" she was asking.

Paul faced her. The pit of his stomach contracted hard. "It was a boy," he said.

"Boy!"

"Yes, seems like a nice kid," he said.

"Is Sue . . . ." His wife's hand fluttered helplessly. "Is she keen on him . . . ?"

"Looks like it," Paul said. "At least, they're going dancing tonight."

For a second, Alice thought she had not heard him correctly. She sat back on the edge of the table, staring at him.

"Tonight?" she echoed. Surely he had not given permission for Susan to go unchaperoned. But he was nodding.

"Seems the boy has a car. He'll be up after dinner." Alice turned away from him, struggling with her dread.

Didn't he realize Susan was . . . was slow? Why did the mother have to carry all the responsibility?

In the most normal voice she could muster she said "Where is he from?" And silently she added, And who is he, and where does he go to school, and how old is he, and is he kind?

"She didn't tell me," Paul was saying. "But his name's Drew, Jimmy Drew. Helps on the soft drink truck."

For a flickering moment Alice was sure she would drop the tray. Paul's hand guided it through the crisis.

"Paul, you can't be serious."

He set down the tray for her. "Look dear," he said gently, "it's only to be expected. She works in a diner. Her boy works on a supply truck."

"But she doesn't *have* to work there."

"She does have to, it's good for her, gives her self-confidence," Paul said.

Alice put the worst of her fears into words. "Does he look intelligent?"

Paul laughed, reached out to her and gave her an overplayful buss on the cheek.

"I didn't give him an I.Q. test, but he looks like every other kid of his age." And what did that mean? Alice asked herself. Only that this boy had bristly hair and a negligent manner.

The clatter of Susan's door jolted her nerves. She turned to see her daughter rushing downstairs holding her hands out stiffly, like a burns victim.

"Oh dear, oh Mommy, it went all over my fingers."

She ran to Alice and showed fingernails daubed sloppily with vivid nail polish. Alice felt her face relaxing into a smile. Every woman secretly wanted her children to remain young and dependent forever. This was the one compensation Susan's handicap held. She gave her daughter a quick hug. "Go, wipe your fingers with the remover, I'll do your nails later," she said.

"But I won't have time!" Sue squealed. "I gotta date."

"Count on me," her mother assured her.

Alice turned to call Kay in from the patio. They ate, and for once Susan was not hungry. Kay entertained them with an account of some boy recently transferred from a western university. Somehow Kay's talk seemed so unnecessarily brittle, Alice thought. Why could her daughters' intelligence levels not have averaged out more fairly?

As soon as the meal ended Susan pushed back from the table, abandoning her chair where it stood.

"How about my nails?" she demanded.

Kay jerked her head up in surprise. "Going out?"

Alice shared the victory in Susan's reply.

"Gotta date," Sue said.

"Well, good for you." Kay biffed her sister on the back. She should have hidden her astonishment, Alice thought. They must not bruise Susan's shiny new confidence.

"What time is your boy calling?" Alice asked.

Susan's chin dropped. "He said after supper, but I don't know when he eats supper," she moaned.

"Then let's go," Kay said. "Come on, you can borrow my blue dress." She led the way, up the stairs. Alice stood at the stair rail, nursing her fear. Who was this boy Susan was dressing to please? Was he fond of her, despite her handicap, or because it would make her an easy mark?

She waited almost without moving, until Susan came out of Kay's room, irresistible as a kitten in a new bow. Alice extended both hands to her daughter. "Why, honey, you're beautiful," she whispered and it was true. There was a new, womanly depth to Susan's eyes, a subtle bloom on her personality.

"I was going to wear my pink," she said shyly.

"That rag!" Kay dismissed it. "You're a knockout, sister dear. Just don't take any chances with the boy friend."

"Kay!" Alice rapped out her disapproval but Kay shrugged it away.

"You sure rubbed that point in when I went out first," she said.

175

"That was different."

"It certainly was," Kay said. She turned and went back to her room to prepare for her own date.

Paul was sitting in his deep chair, opposite the window. "Looks like a car coming," he said. Susan gave an injured flutter of her arms and rushed to the window.

"Soun's like Jimmy's," she said, "his car's gotta real good motor."

Let it not be Jimmy, Alice prayed. Let it be some stranger, some knight from a story, some prince.

Beside her, Susan's profile was worried, questing, then it melted into a smile. "That's him."

Alice exchanged a horrified glance with her husband. The twenty-year-old coupé that roared up the driveway was painted scarlet. Twin fox tails fluttered from the aerial. It pulled up crisply beside Paul's car and the youth slid out. He was husky, even attractive, but his clothes! Alice gasped; a roll-necked shirt, slim black pants with a wide leather belt—to her, he seemed outlandish.

As Alice watched he ran up the steps. Then she heard the front door flung open and Susan's voice said, "Hi, Jimmy, I been ready ages."

Alice clicked along the hallway to the door. "Do come in," she said and the boy stood back to allow Susan to go first.

Paul carried out the introduction. "Hi, Jimmy, glad you could make it. Dear, this is Jimmy Drew—Jimmy, this is Susan's mother." The boy stuck out his hand, then made an uncomfortable gesture when he realized Alice was not going to shake.

"Glad to know you, Mis' Wheatley," he said.

"How do you do," Alice smiled; but Drew just grimaced awkwardly. Kay had flounced in from the sitting-room. She smiled at Jimmy and he bobbed his head, holding his back stiff, like an unskilled actor.

Alice found her mouth puckering wordlessly as she tried to set out the limitations to Susan's date. "We'd like Susan home by eleven thirty," she managed, but her husband overruled her with, "It's the biggest part of half an hour's drive to Claremont, dear. I think Sue can play Cinderella for this once."

Stay out till midnight, with this stranger, was her husband

losing his senses? Alice fumed. But before she could put her anxiety into words he was ushering the couple to the door. "Midnight then, eh?" he was saying. "Sure thing," Jimmy said.

Couldn't he see this was a sacrifice on their part? Alice thought. Had he no sensitivity? She joined her husband at the door. "Have fun." The words clung in a whisper to her dry lips.

"'Bye Mom, 'bye Dad." Susan looked up at them, then ran down the steps. Drew followed her, and it seemed to Alice that his eyes never left the firm lines of her daughter's body. She clutched Paul's arm. They watched while Drew opened the driver's door, slid across the seat and twisted the door open for Susan. Paul's chuckle was forced. "I thought for a moment he was going without her," he said.

Alice tightened her grip on his arm. As the old, old car drove down the driveway, she was saying, "It's nonsense, Paul. She has nothing in common with him."

His lips pursed before he spoke. "Let the kid live," he said. "He's all right."

Alice felt the frustrated tears tingling behind her eyelids. "From the first moment the other girls brought fellows home I liked them," she said. "They've always been polite, decent boys. This one is from Cabbagetown. He's just awful."

"He seems to think Susan's worth knowing," Paul argued, "and that's the kind of backing she needs."

Alice could have clutched her husband by the lapels and shaken him. "Why couldn't she meet someone nice, like Kay's boy, or like Ella's husband?"

Paul straightened up tall. "Listen to me," he was almost hissing. "Susan is a sweet, pretty kid but she's got an I.Q. of barely 80. If she's lucky, very very lucky, she'll meet someone just a little brighter. Then he'll feel protective towards her, never resentful."

Alice felt helpless anger welling up within her. She wanted to scream that this was a time for love and understanding, not analysis. But her husband didn't read her face, he was going on and on, as if he had planned the speech years before and waited his chance to deliver it.

"The worst kind of boy for her would be someone like Kay's

fellow. He'd take her out because he pitied her. Within a week he'd be ashamed of her and himself . . . ."

Alice kept her voice icy. "No doubt you know best about that kind of thing. Personally, I'm not an expert on male motivations. I happen to be a mother and I happen to know what's best for my child."

"Do you?" Paul turned to face her, his fists clenched, arms locked rigidly against his sides.

"Do you?" He asked it again and his own bitterness made his body tremble like a cord drawn too tight.

"Who kept her on at school until she started crying herself to sleep at nights? Who took her on those dreadful holidays?" He made the word sound obscene. Alice felt her colour leave her face but she didn't sway, didn't speak. She let the words break over her like the waters of a long-awaited storm. Paul slackened his arms and slowly brought his hands together in front of him. "Remember? Tagging her along like a pet poodle into places that bored or scared or humiliated her? Tagging her along like an operation scar that you could show in public." His voice sank down to a whisper. "There have been times when I honestly thought you were glad you had something in this family to grieve over."

"How dare you." The words forced themselves from between her clenched teeth, and once they started she couldn't stop. "How dare you! How dare you!"

His face was distorted through the prism of her tears but she did not weep.

"Tell me this then, Mister Wonderful . . . ." She could see him again clearly now. "Who flew her to Montreal to the neurologists? Who refused to accept the verdict that anybody could see was true, anybody with half an eye?"

"I did." Paul pushed his right hand through his hair and back over his head until he was holding fiercely to the back of his neck. Alice guessed he must be hurting himself and a part of her felt sorry for him.

"Penfield is the best man on the continent. I wanted to do the best for her. It was ridiculous but at least it was concrete. I wasn't doing it because I felt sorry for myself."

"And I suppose you mean I was," Alice said.

"Forget it." Paul turned away. "It's something we've got to live with."

"I've lived with it for seventeen years." Alice felt her eyes beginning to well with tears and she shook her head angrily. "And I guess I'll live with it for the rest of my life."

Paul said "Yes, I guess you will. So have a good weep. And then think about Sue. She's going to live with it, too."

"I know. What kind of a selfish monster do you think I am? I've put her first in everything. The school, the hospitals, the holidays. Do you think I enjoyed it all?"

"Maybe not but it helped you feel a little less guilty." Paul bit the words off sharp.

For a second Alice thought she hadn't heard correctly. The words hung in her brain like separated beads of sound. Slowly the meaning became clear.

"Are you saying I felt guilty about Susan?"

Paul said nothing. He looked away, head low. Alice repeated the question.

"Are you? Are you?" Slowly she felt herself rocking backwards and forwards on her heels and her voice rose and suddenly she was beating her fists against his back. "Are you blaming me for the way Susan is? Answer me."

He whirled and seized her hands, gripping her wrists until she could have cried out from the pain.

"You could have been at that hospital an hour earlier. You could have had her like you'd had the others. But no. You had to race the stork. You'd been through it twice before. Remember? Only this time you lost and the taxi driver wasn't much of a midwife and he forgot to start her breathing in time. Remember?"

He threw down her hands, swallowing his words. His eyes were glinting with the first tears Alice could ever remember seeing there.

Slowly, like a robot she slapped his face. His head spun sideways from the force of it but he didn't speak for a long moment. Then he said, "I'm glad you did that. I apologize."

And it was now, when words might have helped, that he could no longer speak. His face burning from the slap, he felt the sentences roll into his brain, silently.

179

He should never have made the accusation. Not because it was false—possibly it was true—but because it was useless now. The damage was done and had been a part of their lives for so long that no purpose could be served by wondering. Wondering was only indulging in the worst sin of all: self-pity.

He was powerless to stop his wife as she moved slowly away from him towards the door.

He turned and followed her as she walked up the stairs to their bedroom and sat down dully at the dressing table.

There, standing over her, looking down at her greying hair, he found his voice.

"I'm sorry."

If she heard, she gave no sign. Her hand reached slowly for the hairbrush. Paul knelt, pressing his face into her shoulder, trying to bury his anguish. "It was an idiotic thing to say. Pointless and cruel. I wouldn't have said it if I wasn't at the end of my tether."

She ignored him, her shoulder moved rhythmically, almost soothingly, as she began brushing her hair.

Paul pulled his face back from her, far enough to speak clearly. "I don't expect you to forgive me. I just want you to know I'm going to make up for it, somehow."

She made no gesture of recognition. Paul dipped his face to the side of her neck and kissed her quickly. "I'll make it right," he repeated. Then he stood up and walked out of the room, knowing what he had to do.

Alice did not leave their room. Paul half expected her to appear as he sat on the patio chair smoking away the hours until Susan's return. He made his plan, he chose the words he would use, sharpened them as he would have done for a board meeting, then changed his mind, and dulled the message down to its least subtle form.

At last he heard the boy's old car vibrating on the night silence: he got up and checked the time. It was twenty-five to one. Drew had failed Susan then. Paul went through the silent house to the front door. He opened it to find Susan on the top step. She had Drew's coat about her shoulders, and he was standing behind her, one pace away. Paul said, "You're awful late, Sue."

Her head dropped and she looked away; what degree of guilt was she hiding? Paul wondered. Then Drew said, "I'm sorry, Mister Wheatley." Paul looked at him in surprise. There was a smudge of black grease across one cheekbone.

"What happened?" he asked. The boy came up the extra step and indicated with his hands an invisible object about the size of a football.

"Like I have twin carbs on there, see, one for each bank o' cylinders." There was an expert earnestness to his words. "I've been havin' trouble with one, the float sticks, it floods all the time." His hands were stained with the same underhood grime, Paul noticed. He was continuing. "That's what happened. We came out of the dance in plenty 'a time, but the car wouldn't start. I had to strip the carb down right there in the lot." He nodded to Susan. "Sue held the light for me—it made us late."

Paul turned to Sue. She was looking at him with almost superstitious awe. "I'm sorry, Dad. I was going to be home early," she said. Paul reached out and ran his finger along the line of her jaw.

"I understand, kitten," he said. "You go in and get ready for bed." She gasped with release. "G'night, Jimmy." She handed the coat back. The boy offered his shoulder for her to drop it on, waving his filthy hands to show his predicament. Paul took the jacket. "Here, let me put it in your car," he said. Drew nodded casually, looking straight past him at Susan. "G'night, Sue." He hesitated in embarrassment then added, "I had a good time."

"Me too," Susan said. "See you tomorrow." She waved at him with her fingers, and turned away into the house. Drew stared at the door for a mesmerized second longer, then pattered down the steps toward his car. Paul walked beside him priming himself for his speech.

He twisted open the door of the car and dropped the jacket across the seat. Drew was at his elbow. Paul leaned on the top of the open car door, and cleared his throat.

"This is kind of hard to say, Jimmy," he began. The boy waited. Paul altered his line of approach, backing down before the silent challenge.

181

"How d'you make out in your present job, does it pay?" he asked.

"Two dollars an hour," Drew said, his voice puzzled. "I work forty hours most weeks."

Paul dug his fingers into his hair, slowly, as if thinking. "And you have a chauffeur's license?"

"Right," Jimmy said. "I'll likely get a route of my own next year. That pays real good."

"Well, listen"—Paul rushed into his speech—"we need a driver at the plant. Just a light delivery run. Pays one hundred and ten plus for a forty-hour week."

"You mean I could get that?" The boy's voice rose.

"You could, with a little pushing from me," Paul said. He cleared his throat again. "Course, you'd be working out the West End."

"That'd be fine." The boy sounded bemused until Paul added his final words.

"I mean you'd never get around to seeing Susan."

Jimmy rubbed his cheek in bewilderment. What was with this guy anyway? Here, he'd just known him a day and he was coming across with a tremendous job. So he could call on Sue nights, lots of guys never saw their girls till night anyway.

"I could get to see her nights," he said. Mr. Wheatley's face tilted down towards him, and suddenly the whole plan was obvious.

"I'd kind of appreciate it if you didn't," he said.

Jimmy felt his fists tighten into an itching knot. If this man wasn't Sue's dad, he'd get a punch in the mouth right now. What kind of talk was this anyway?

"Why'd you say that, I ain't done nothing to Sue." His voice ran away on him, rising angrily.

Sue's father didn't know what to say, Jimmy thought. He plunged on with gathering confidence. "What have you got against me?"

"Nothing." Paul's voice was flat, weary.

"I can tell you what it is," Jimmy said. "Jus' because this junker of mine's twenny years old, instead of being a new Oldsmobile, you got me figured for a bum. Well, let me tell you something, Mister. I've got money saved, plenty of it." No need telling him how much, but three hundred dollars was a pretty big sum for a guy of nineteen who had to keep himself in lodgings and clothes and all.

"It isn't the money, Jim," Paul said, "it's just that Sue isn't like her sisters. She's not ready to go seriously with a fellow."

"So what's serious?" Drew demanded. "We went to a dance, had a few laughs."

Paul's words broke from him in an exasperated rush. "She's slow, Jimmy. She isn't bright like her sisters."

Jimmy relaxed his fists and stretched one index finger towards Paul. "Now listen, Mister," he said. "Don't you start calling her down to me. I talk to her every day at work. She's about the nicest girl I ever met. So don't say nothing about her to me." In the light from the porch he saw Mr. Wheatley shrug his shoulders. Then the low, almost pleading voice began again.

"I'm telling you, she has a problem that needs all the care and attention that we can give her. Maybe one of these days she'll be ready to date boys, but not yet awhile."

Drew smacked his hands together fiercely. "You're tryin' to tell me she's stupid. That's it, isn't it?" he asked. The man nodded.

This time Jimmy's hard forefinger reached Paul's chest. "Well, let me tell you something," he said. "You only think she's dumb because you and her mother and that sister with the teeth, you figure you're so all-fired smart. I saw you look when I come in earlier. Looking down your noses. You think money means everything. Just because you've got a big house and a fancy car you think you're special." He pushed past Paul and slid into the driver's seat. "Don't worry," he said, "I won't be around here no more. And you can keep your job, I don't need that kind of help from nobody." Even as he said it he was regretting his words. An extra thirty a week would be good, no doubt of that. He still had to find his rent every week, and ship a couple of dollars back East to the old lady. Thirty dollars more would be useful. But he wasn't going to stand any pushing around for it, that was for sure. "Thanks for nothing," he said and hooked the door shut, jolting Paul's elbow off the top.

Paul regained his balance as the car waffled into life. The boy backed it out with insolent skill and spurted down the driveway. Paul stood watching the tail lights diminishing as the car turned down the highway. What had he done? He slapped his hands against his cheeks. Whatever the kid's faults, he was completely honourable in his intentions to Susan. He liked . . . perhaps loved her, and now he was driving away hating everything that surrounded her.

Paul stopped pacing and stared around, taking stock of the environment they had bought, yes, bought, when they learned about Susan—the conventional, discreet "house in the country." The night scents of the garden, the substantial bulk of the house, the gently tracery of the trees against the sky; it all said warmth, and love . . . and money, he admitted grimly. Maybe the boy was right.

Slowly he walked into the house. He could hear Susan's voice from the kitchen, singing the meaningless lyrics of a popular song. He stopped. There was a womanly subtlety to the singing that was foreign to him; Susan must be crazy about this boy. He sucked in a deep breath and went on up the stairs. Alice sat up and clicked on her light.

"Is Susan home?" She was rosy with sleep, infinitely soft.

"Yes, got in a while ago." He pulled off his shoes, deliberately keeping his back to her. "I had a word with the boy," he said, not turning his head. Alice's voice ran up the scale in ascending interest. "Oh, what about?"

Paul let his shoes drop, then turned to face her, biting his lip.

"I offered him a better job, a job at our place. It would mean he didn't get to see Susan through the day."

"And did he take it?"

Paul wished he had said nothing, but continued. "He said he could come and see her at nights, and I told him we'd appreciate it if he didn't."

Suddenly Alice was sitting bolt upright. "You mean you bought him off."

"Well, I tried to," he said. "I was trying to make things like they were before today." His eyes had dropped from his wife's face, and her voice burned into him.

"You mean you deliberately spoiled Susan's friendship because of what you said to me earlier this evening?"

"That's it, I guess," Paul said. It was curious the way a woman

184

could be so blind in so many ways, yet able to strip all pretence from an important fact.

He threw down the shoe he had unlaced. "I was trying to do the best for her," he said.

Alice found herself looking at him, as if he were some stranger at the scene of an accident. He looked up as she stepped out of bed, swooping up her housecoat, and walked down to the kitchen.

Susan was sitting in the breakfast nook with a glass of milk, her little radio propped before her. She was resting her cheek on one fist, her eyes filled with the familiar mistiness, and she did not hear her mother enter.

"Did you have fun, kitten?" Alice slid into the seat opposite her daughter.

"Oh, Mommy, I had a ball, honest." You would believe her to be perfectly normal tonight, Alice thought—a teenager in the first tremors of love. For an infinite moment Alice recalled how her own heart had danced the night she had sat in Susan's place. The boy—she could not even remember what he looked like, and yet the impression he had left on her emotions was larger than life itself. With a new gentleness she extended her hand and touched Susan's clenched fingers.

"Is he really nice?" she whispered.

Susan rocked her head in abandonment. "He's awful nice, Mom. He held my hand." Alice patted the curled fingers. How innocent and fragile Susan's world was tonight. That ordinary boy was something almost mystical to her. Alice was suddenly ashamed of her early fears. And now it was too late. Susan's house of cards had been sent fluttering. Alice stood up, angry at the tears which teased along her eyelids.

"Better hurry to bed, dear," she said. "Work tomorrow." Susan finished her milk, spilling a little as she picked the glass up. Then she took up her radio, still playing, and sleepily waltzed towards the stairs. Alice stared after her. On this magic night it was impossible to tell which of her daughters this was. All the femininity of the whole human race danced in Susan's shoes. Alice stood at the bottom stair, grateful tears filling her eyes. "Goodnight, darling," she whispered.

She walked slowly up after Susan and back to the bedroom. Paul was motionless, hugging sleep to him like a cover. Alice wanted to wake him and shout the news of their daughter's miracle. But she pitied his guilt and let him sleep on.

By morning, no trace of the spell remained. Susan was grumpy from lack of sleep. Paul did not speak, and Kay did not even come down for breakfast. Only Alice, aching with insomnia, remembered the mood. She finished breakfast and said, "I'll run you down to work, Sue." Paul looked up at her.

"I can do it," he said.

"I'll do it," Alice repeated. He looked at her again, then lowered his face.

"O.K."

Alice backed her nimble little English car out of the garage. "Hurry dear, or we'll be late," she chivvied. Susan said only, "Why can't we go in Dad's car? It's gotta radio."

"Maybe tonight." Alice plunged along the driveway.

There were no cars waiting at the diner, only the jangling hulk of the soft drink delivery truck. Alice pulled in beside it, looking around for Drew. Susan said, "That's Jimmy's truck. I guess he's inside."

She pushed the door open and swung out of the car. Alice switched off the ignition and followed her into the diner. Jimmy was straightening up from his pile of wooden pop crates. He had his back to the door, but it seemed to Alice that there was a new grimness about him. The driver of the truck was with him, and he extended an aluminum-backed order book towards Susan.

"Twelve dozen king size. Put your X here, gorgeous."

Susan took the pencil and scrawled her name in the book. She was looking at Jimmy's back. Alice silently prayed for the boy to turn around but he stacked his crates without any sign of awareness. The driver snapped his book shut and headed past Alice towards the door.

"You get your coffee now, Romeo," he said to Drew. "I'll pick ya' up on the way back from the burger joint."

Now Drew straightened. "Don' worry, I'm with you," he said. Then he saw Alice and dropped his eyes. Susan was saying, "Aren't you gonna have a coffee?" running her words together into a slithering whine. Drew looked at her, then past her, at Alice.

"I don't feel like coffee today," he said. He walked to the door as it swung to behind his driver. Alice took an urgent step to the left, guarding the door.

"Please," she said. The boy stopped and looked at her, down at her, she noticed. "Please, Jimmy," she said again. He pulled in his lip.

"Another job offer, I guess," he said and Alice shrank from his bitterness. She put out her hand and touched his arm. "Let's have some coffee," she said, and steered him into a booth. "I wanted to apologize, Jimmy," she said.

He turned his head away and fanned down her words with an angry hand. "Save your breath."

She had known this would not be easy, Alice reminded herself. She said, "If I could have reached you last night, I would have, and so would Susan's father."

"What broke him down?" Drew asked. "He played it cool when I was up at the house."

"I know. It's just that we didn't know what the score was with you and Susan." Alice found herself clutching the comfortable, convenient lie. She choked down her deeper feminine explanations and said, "I know it was unfair, but we were sort of testing you."

"Look, lady, I don't have to jump through hoops to go out with any chick," Drew said.

"I know that, but we feel an extra responsibility towards Susan." Alice sought for some euphemism but the boy made it unnecessary. "Yeah, her father told me about that too, and if you ask me, it's him got the head trouble, not Susan. Leastways she knows how to talk straight." Alice felt the colour rising in her face; this fresh kid . . . ! But already he was adding "I don't mean any offence, mind. It's just I don't like people saying things about her, even if they are her folks."

Alice felt her hand move of itself across the table. Her voice pitched itself lower than she could control as she said, "That's the nicest thing I've ever heard a boy say, about any girl."

She saw the boy's shoulders dip uncomfortably but with a grace that pleased her; it became a motion, in time to the saraband that had throbbed all night in her brain. Perhaps this boy would be tired of Susan in a week, or perhaps he would be her husband some day. But whatever came of this first affair, Susan was freed from the restrictions imposed by her father's income. Today she was an equal in the family, for the very first time. Alice fumbled for a handkerchief and wiped her eyes. When she looked up again Susan was approaching the table with two cups of coffee. Alice said, "Dear, I was just inviting Jimmy to come up for dinner some night soon, tonight if he can."

The boy had reached for the sugar jar and begun to tilt it over his cup. At Alice's words he stopped and pushed the jar to her, with remembered politeness. "That would be swell, Mrs. Wheatley," he said. "Tonight would be just fine."